# What the Farmer Told the Bard, a Novel of Erotic Panpsychism

G—Gar, the rune of Gungnir, Odin's spear.

# WHAT THE FARMER TOLD THE BARD

## A Novel of Erotic Panpsychism

Third Edition

Paul V. Cornell du Houx

☙ ❧

Polar Bear & Company
An imprint of the
Solon Center for Research and Publishing
Solon & Rockland, Maine

Polar Bear & Company is an imprint of the
Solon Center for Research and Publishing
PO Box 311, Solon, ME 04979, USA.
polarbearandco.org, soloncenter.org

Polar Bear & Company books are available at local bookstores in many countries, or online, or at info@soloncenter.org.
Retailers may order via Ingram.
ISBN: 978-1-959112-05-1
Third paperback edition first printed 2023

Second paperback edition, revised, 2020

Library of Congress Control Number: 2019956050
First published in 1996 in paperback as *Indian Summer: The Return of the Myth of the Running Man*, ISBN 978-1-882190-44-7



By permission of the Folger Shakespeare Library: the illustration of the engraving of the Shakespeare Monument, attributed to Wenceslaus Hollar, published in *Antiquities of Warwickshire* by Sir William Dugdale. Cover design with bind-rune and birch bark, by author.

For more on the anthropology of the Running Christ and other traditional stories and symbols: John Bierhorst trilogy, including *The Mythology of North America; The Mythology of South America; The Mythology of Mexico and Central America* (William Morrow and Company, Inc.); *Ogam Consaine and Tifinag Alphabets: Ancient Uses*, by Warren W. Dexter (Academy Books).



Manufactured on durable, acid-free paper in more than one country.

# Contents



ଓଃ ଛ

Shakespeare Monument engraving, attributed to Wenceslaus Hollar, *Antiquities of Warwickshire* by Sir William Dugdale

# Illustrations



ଓ ଉ

Th—Thurisaz, rune of thorns, the gateway.

# Prologue

JUST ARRIVED THROUGH A PORTHOLE, I strolled along the fields, as though the back of a cave had opened out. It was a land new to me, so I stopped in conversation with a farmer. I asked a few questions that might seem mundane to a traveler, like where am I? What time is it? What year?

The farmer took it philosophically and brought out the hard cider. I complimented her on the strong, straight maize in the field. She looked at me directly and said that it was strange, given that it was still springtime.

She hailed a dog that was trying to run a man off the property and down the road. She smiled, then laughed out loud in spite of herself. Slightly unnerved, I said I should be getting along now and turned to leave. But she gave me a look of reassurance, and we fell into conversation. Every so often I made to resume my travels, but each time she would entreat me to stay. "Why the hurry?" she finally asked. Eventually, she told me this tale, which I will retell—in my own way, of course.

B—Berkano, rune of Freya, feminine energy, love, fertility, the birch tree, rebirth.

# 1. The Love Triangle

JOHN, THE PHOTOGRAPHER, WAS MOVING ROUND the standing stone, where she posed like a temple dancer who awakens the sensual memory.

"So . . . that's what they were like!" An unbreathed thought slipped out through the parted lips of the inventor, Jesús de l'Orient, leaving him hesitant.

Just then, after the few soft clicks of a single lens reflex, each precisely preset and yet, inspirationally, sensually separated from each other like the mysterious rhythm of a supple photographic clock, now waiting to be timed again, just then, she sensed the hesitation and posed with finality.

The photographer breathed a sigh in release of the exquisite tension of his art, and again she moved, flowed into an even more suggestive, significant pose.

The time-honored art of feminine expression. She was a true dancer. She held nothing back, she was open. Always, this was it! And now like this— Like this? Now! And now again.

As she moved and the photographer moved around the stone by degrees, the inventor observed how the energy of this motion, with the camera angle and depth of field, moved him.

"What next? What next?" he wondered. "And who invented what? What led to my thoughts, my actions and what leads away?

"And what about the One God?"

He focused on Bellarose, the model. He dismissed the God concept outright. It was history now, anyway. He'd been thrown out of the Project.

"Numbskulls!" he muttered, "The All-in-All can go fuck itself! No, it can't. I've got to relax—"

He cooled himself out with the question of how God could be self-fertile. He had to think.

Her stance was so complete. The sex it stirred up in him reminded him of things he couldn't exactly recall experiencing, exotic, familiar, extremely familiar . . . He was hesitating again.

She was sex. Completely nude, nothing at all to distract from her form. No reminders of what era, society, culture or magazine she stepped out of. No reminders of paraphernalia, eternal, except for something in the pose enacted, the inspiration given sensually: there was wisdom, transmitted almost unconsciously on the electric wings of sex. It hit him again with a flash of truth in his center.

Something unending, a hot translucent window into any age, any past experience, any incarnation.

Specifically what, he could not say for sure, but this, he realized, was sexual insight, deepening into flashes of memory that faded like dreams at the touch of his own particular consciousness. He hesitated, feeling almost as though he, too, might fade.

But she was channeling to him nature's hot touch in his essence. And he accepted reincarnation, of course. It was an established fact at the Project. And it was his breakthrough, as though, somehow, the whole thing, even rebirth, was his own invention.

The hardware had been beautifully engineered, the software debugged in the deepest secrecy and perfection. "Does anyone know what's happening?" he wondered. "And am I only now realizing the impact of a scientific fact?"

She was so completely without any clothes and so natural a woman that she could appear clothed and yet nude at the same time, as though a pre-Christian animal spirit graced her form. Here was a great natural cat, a cat-woman, as the term would have been understood by a forgotten civilization, the poetry and history, today, emptied out, leaving an objectified cliché until a Bellarose comes along, and all the comedy of cats jumps back into everyday life, along with all the rest, and once more it's perfectly clear that there are still cat-women like there used to be, once or twice before.

Here was one of those who could make clothing look absurd. And the people in the clothing might look as though they had such a fear and a respect for the garments off the rack that they would go about their affairs rack-like, so the clothes on their backs and legs would not be too disturbed.

"If the weather's warm, we should take them off," she would say. "It's natural for a woman to be admired by the male sex."

The world, as he was used to it, often began to feel like heavy clothing on a hot day when he was with her. Now he was back, hesitating, even though this was it—and he had finally returned. And it must be love that had brought him back.

He reached back for that newly rediscovered atmosphere, the sexual history of their relationship. What about John? He reached back some more, feeling for the times they had all three been together. How much credit should it be given, he wondered and hesitated some more, watching for any recrimination, any credit in return, any hesitation or guilt.

Her breasts, the mandalas, focused him back through the ages with their subtle power suddenly to project the whole live history of humanity: It was just like this, yes, even then, in those days—but they moved a little more like so—and the sun was hotter, and the skin was a little more brown. The light seemed to change, and her skin was now darker. He recognized her all over. It was still she, but the name, he had forgotten it. Forgotten it recently, as well.

He focused on her mandalas in this temple dance, now in profile, a loving shape that brought out the fullness of her lips, relaxed in an obsolete language that shocked him just then with its proximity, that it might speak through to the present century, and he might understand what she was saying, as he used to without thinking.

She was speaking like water in water's moon language, filling him with the knowledge that he really ought to be able to speak this universal tongue as well, to understand it.

It was clear, but he listened for something more specific. He shuddered at the emptiness in overblown generalities that might collapse him into a foolish, washed-out cartoon, drowning. How specific could nature be? He wondered, held his breath and listened to the nearby stream. "Where water goes? Can I hear her soul? Do I have the power?"

She rocked her hips and barely winked at him. He was taken by surprise. What could she know? "No!" he thought, "She's just merging, channeling it—"

It flowed, danced through her, with her, charged her with its electric streams that confirmed honesty and completeness. No interference, no paraphernalia, and no clothes now!

He followed the line of her thighs to the climactic letter *Y*, famous for spelling ultimates, firing rivers of multicolored energy to dance on the hills. He had monitored those colors on screen. He had written the programs that could break down social, sexual, human programs, and he was the one—but they had established the Project, the Light Centers, and thrown him out. He—the inventor, the architect, the creator, out!

But now, again, he watched amazed, as her dark hair fell and curled lightly above the curve of her hips. She was facing away from him at an angle, towards the camera.

Then she stepped over to the standing stone and sat down. She arched her back, raised her arms upwards and outwards, inviting the sky down between her breasts and releasing tension to fly clear, while she watched and felt the exchange of energy emphasize the landscape with its pressures, its statement.

The camera reemphasized it. It was a wave, the flexible moment fixed in light-sensitive data, to be worked, reworked and printed on the hard copy, the stone struck by water, the pebble into water, setting up wave motion in time, supple, photographic, a clock in motion, timing the surrounding events, timed by the next shutter release in conjunction with her pose in the landscape.

She spread her thighs out towards him, and the inside angles with her calves swept down her ankles like lightning along her feet pointing with sex, curving the wave off the angles and into the ground, where it merged with the root of the stone. The photographer gently pressed the stone and the image of her pose, like a word spoken into a wave: acupressure of the landscape. It was their relationship, launched into an invisible stream by the gods.

The inventor had discovered those waves, had studied their polarity and knew that Bellarose and John were unblocking the planet, true to nature. But the waves had kept disappearing and disappearing, off screen.

He had further discovered how little the couple knew or could see of their work. And he had felt the effects at the Project. It had shown up clearly. The system had allowed him to watch those waves change in amplitude, catalytically in conjunction with surrounding events and then politically at close hand, more so now that he was here.

He had tried to calculate how much was due to his personal involvement.

He had discovered that those waves, small in many respects, were historic in their reach, like the effects of the invention of the printing press and the consequent spread of a language, powered by what his father had referred to as "Shakespeare's word."

He had grown up with this "word." It was a bittersweet thing, he had finally realized, born into a noble family, that this word had, it seemed, been the last word on an entire cherished way of life.

One small word like "monarch," for example, would never again ring right since that bard, in English. So, he was part French . . . and Spanish, his father would remind him. He was expected to appreciate some ghostly irony here, some sort of an inside joke. The initiates would always eye him for the correct response. He still didn't know what the hell they were on about.

"Shakespeare's word? Perhaps, perhaps, be as it may—" he would think to himself, "I'm just the computer jock, heir to the printer's apprentice."

Now, standing there, he realized that this woman's flexible pose, this pictogram sent into nature by sun and moon, would be absent without him. She would still pose, but the words would be different. He had returned. It was a love triangle.

He hunted that lost name, transfixed at the sight of her reaching out to the sun, hands cupped with the flood of its rays, breasts fully presented by the arch of her back, the flow of her neck, the accent of her jaw, the inhaling line of her nose, the flare of eyes, the taste of lips and the ever-extending smooth flood and rush of her thighs to the angle of her knees and into the ground, to the tip of the empty pyramid filled by the continuously standing stone between her legs, coloring the upper and inner thighs with creams and pinks with the upward pressure on her lifting body, sending sex into the mound, the heather-scented tor of curling hair, rising full of texture, awaiting caress, his caress, he realized, slowly, in flashes, as he listened to the supple photographic clock.

She glanced at the line of the erection in his blue jeans and licked her parted lips. She leaned all the way back, placing one hand on the stone, the other presenting the sky as though to bring memory to light. As though it had been a sky like this, a day such as this, her flood of hair catching the sun and following the heat down to the wide surface of the stone. All the way back she stretched, opening up the lips, red, wet and wild between her thighs.

He felt an electric tang of saliva remind him in an instant of the vastness of lifetimes and the excitement that, yet again, this was it.

He watched her raise her hips briefly, heard one more soft shutter release and she was up off the stone, standing, shaking comically her tail and fanning her pubic hair, rocking her hips, "Hooo, wow, hot! Horny!"

She looked back at the still-standing stone where a wet spot glistened in its ancient crystals with the sun.

He advanced. He felt in tune with the event and with something wild but precise, as though they were three parts of a living sundial, where they stood among the stones on a farm in central Maine, by the Kennebec River. "We could have sex here—" he ventured, having halted just out of reach.

"I feel like we just have," she turned to John, "don't you?"

He beamed at her. She rounded on the inventor, "Well then, Jesús!" She moved her hands over her hips. "You've come a long way! Are you just going to stand there?"

The inevitable, the wave again, was happening. He was going to kiss her. It shocked him as it passed, and he almost feared the next.

She and John were married, and they were following through. He was joining them. Or was he? He pulled back. The artificiality of the gesture slapped him with the backlash—that wave again!

He was here because of it; he'd figured that one out, days ago. It would backlash him with his own hypocrisy, little by little in their company, until it slapped him all the way back to Switzerland, back into one of those cocktail poses, holding the martini or spinning the ice ironically in the whisky glass, an ignoramus, one of the brothers.

No, either they flowed together in this triangle, he figured, or they all risked destruction like any friends who get closer and closer, naturally sharing love, meanwhile trying to pretend otherwise, as though there's no all-round desire for sex, while the triangle generates its famous geometric heat by degrees of consent in subtle gestures and tone of voice—denied and denied, he figured, until they have to behave as though there is no quagmire, no cynicism and hypocrisy, no nihilism. OK, so they wanted the truth! He would show them. That's the way it was with this couple. Hence the waves. So, he too would be a wave. At least!

Forced by his own science to admit to himself, in his most private cupboard, that they were for real, he had returned to be in love, with romance!

He touched the softness above her hips with both palms. It was recognition, and the backlash sailed away. They seemed to know each other so well, he thought. This could not be the first time, he was certain. This was the science!

He felt the aura of her breasts approach with those familiar pools of her widening contact, and the mound of Venus would rock just so against his erection, until they kissed. He was so sure.

They kissed on the wave. Then it was as though she was a stranger, and they had slid off screen. Then another wave brought the recognition of pure sex.

He stopped to check his credibility, like he used to, before he'd boogie his image to the sounds of rock 'n' roll.

L—Laguz, rune of water, fluidity.

## 2. The Pebble

THE TALL GRASS AMONG THE GIANT stones invited them to form a circle. They sat down under a hot, clear sky and went silently lazy. Bellarose took the strip of cloth she had cut from an old Indian sari and slowly brought it over her shoulders and tied it round the back. They watched her spread it to near transparency like a fan over each breast. She was already wearing the totally short and frayed cut-offs. Finally John said, "So what's the invention?"

It sounded like a challenge, and he was about to try again to give it another spin, when Jesús stopped him. "Here, I'm sure you'll recognize it. It's simple, take my hands."

They felt uncomfortable. It reminded them of the New Age.

"Is this something from the Project?" she inquired.

"No—" He shrugged patiently.

They held hands in the circle.

"Good, now relax. There, feel your center, feel it in an ocean of energy. Now feel your sexuality in that ocean, feel the energy run through us, the sex is uniting us with its polarity."

Suddenly, as if on impulse, he squeezed John's hand.

"You felt that, if I'm not mistaken?"

"Obviously!"

Jesús smiled. "Bellarose, did you feel me squeeze John's hand?"

There was a moment of silence.

"Of course!"

"But not the way John did, right?"

"Right!"

"You felt it deeply, beyond just registering it visually. There's energy circulating among us because we are conscious. No consciousness, no flow of energy in nature. We've all thought about it. Is it true? That's what I set out to discover."

"We all did!" said John.

"Now I want you and Bellarose to kiss."

John looked at him suspiciously.

"Ah!" the inventor continued. "You feel the energy? Don't let go of my hands. There! Feel it change? Ah, now—"

"Now you're the reluctant lover," said the cat.

John leaned over and kissed her.

"Well, basically, energy flows with male-female polarity, including LGBTQ+ attractions. It's sexual and, to some degree, it's conscious. The question is, to what degree, eh?" He smiled at them. Then ducked his head and shrugged slightly as though to avoid something.

"What about electrons, protons—neutrons," she said. "Has Jesus been dabbling in panpsychism?"

They would sometimes play with his name in English, as though searching for something forgotten with a casual interest, probing him and sometimes finding him surprisingly ticklish; at other times he would suddenly go cold. "Do we want to hold hands? No?" He released them and smiled with determination. "No sex? Quite the contrary. For one thing, folks, in the neutron, we've discovered, there's no true neutrality!"

He raised a finger in parody of the professor. "In fact, all particles have what amounts to a sensual—that's sexual—polarity. Sex flows in and among them. It's conscious." He looked at them and smiled again.

"Wait a minute," said John. "You don't mean this neutron is aware, do you?"

"I don't say it has a soul. No! But I do believe it's about time we scientists acknowledge the other, in fact, the main attraction!" He cocked his head, showing off the blond hair and blue eyes, "All around us in physical nature.

"A tree that is self-fertile, does it actually have a soul? No, I would say, rather, it's the manifestation of nature's polarity in bloom. It's nature's polarity having sex in the form of a tree! Fabulous. But exactly what sort of soul individuality it has is a tough question, to say the least. But it's all consciousness, gravitational consciousness, magnetic consciousness, centrifugal consciousness: all sex, that's the problem."

"Why?" said John.

"You see me here before you, at least, in part, because I told them at the Project that it's probably asleep." He folded his hands and looked humble.

"Probably asleep?" the other echoed lazily.

"Yes, probably, asleep and they fundamentally threw me out, you see?" He smiled.

"Because . . . they don't think it's conscious?"

"No."

"Well, what do they think?"

"They think it's God." His face went blank.

"You told them God is probably asleep?"

"Feel the energy?" said Bellarose.

She looked at him searchingly. "Why did you tell them 'probably'? Maybe they probably threw you out because you said probably!"

"Well, yes, in a way," he shifted the powerful but supple shoulders, "you see, I'm not entirely sure, and to be honest, I said probably. Jack and I ran some statistics. We don't necessarily agree, and things got a little out of hand, but I believe that it is probable that all matter is sleeping consciousness and so God—the All-in-All, as they sometimes call it—is asleep."

"That's what you believe?" said John, grinning, the strong white teeth, the weathered face, the sparkling green eyes, the long hair.

"Yes, it can be demonstrated that He, She or It is most likely not aware of many events. But I really have to describe the technical side a little more, so you understand the political environment, the people running the system. In fact, it got worse."

They waited.

"Yes, well, the problem is, the conscious but sleeping energy that pervades all things, what they are calling God, may not even have enough individuality, that is to say, polarity, to have what one would ordinarily call a soul.

"As it turns out, God is more like the neutron.

"So, I had to tell them, effectively, that probably it didn't have a soul, either, sooo . . ."

"Bellarose is right. You shouldn't have been so honest with these guys, with all those probablys and maybes."

"But the truth is in a machine!"

He looked suddenly desperate, a man whose car won't start.

"It's a strange thing that you're alive," said John.

"Yes, I've been wondering about that, myself."

"Are you sure they threw you out," said Bellarose. "Are you sure you got the ol' heave ho—or was it more like you got the Black Spot and gave them the slip?" She looked him over.

"I'm not sure . . ."

"The soul of honesty," commented John.

Jesús smiled at him defiantly, but teasingly, as though this was a game and John wanted to play, have a little competition. "OK, listen to this, guys. Traces—everything leaves its footprints. Even me!

"The software I designed is capable of identifying a footprint in the sand even long after time has washed its more obvious characteristics away. Because, the thing is, time never washes away anything completely. That footprint is always there to some degree and is, therefore, always remembered. All aspects of nature have a permanent memory because, and here we go again, because all of the natural world is conscious to some degree. Where some forget others may remember for them. A collective unconscious."

"The natural world," John asked, "you mean that to include everything, all matter, the universe, whatever is, like we used to talk about it, like—*it,* right?"

"I think so—"

"So you designed a system that traces all footprints in time?"

"Whoa, go easy! Hang on! Yes and no. The real breakthrough came with the new computer chip.

"Jack calls it the New Neolithic Age. He doesn't like the word 'crystal,' because this technology has special asymmetric characteristics. We just call it 'the glass,' or sometimes 'the goblet.' Glass is transparent, doesn't crystallize, remains disorganized in a quantum balance in motion. So that's when you guys lost track of me. I was carried away by a technology that's so fast it almost had me disappearing without a trace."

There was an awkward silence. John was about to ask more about the computer, but Jesús cut him off. "This was fast beyond anything we could have foreseen. I realized we could run the software . . . Suddenly, it was no longer just a philosophical exercise. We didn't just have our heads in the clouds! It began to happen." He paused, losing the thread.

John spoke, "What you mean is that all those ideas we'd been kicking around and you'd go away and try to record in software languages finally got a ride on the right hardware."

"Suddenly it happened! God, listen you two, listen to what happened.

"Take an object you want to investigate; you want to know its story—take a pebble from the beach, anything! Even a grain of sand . . . or take a photograph! What can it tell you? What's behind the face, and what is the face of the photographer? What relationships brought that picture into being? How well can you see them? Who are they?"

Bellarose stopped him. "First just tell us, how could the system recognize the story told by the pebble, just the simple, living pebble on the beach, OK?"

"The system is fast. The pebble is like one piece of a cosmic puzzle. Its shape is all its own, its crystals are like its personality, they form a pattern, its composition, its energy and so forth. We give the system as much information about the pebble as we can or need to. The system takes it from there. The more pieces of the puzzle we feed in, the fewer the options the system needs to consider in order to work out what the finished puzzle picture looks like. Computers are simple.

"But this is the magic: we, ourselves, can only tell the system very little, hardly anything! It really only adds up to having one piece, one shape in the puzzle to go by, but it can still work through all the pieces fast enough to find the right fit and work out the expanding image of the continuing story of the pebble, as you watch."

"But," said the cat, "couldn't there be a lot of different pieces that fit into the pebble puzzle piece's configuration, giving rise to a lot of different puzzle pictures? How would the system know which was the real one to aim for?"

"Because, and this is, again, the magic, the truth of it all: there is only one true fit, there is only one unique, true environment that, in reality, surrounds and intimately relates to that one and only pebble. It would be impossible to find a connecting piece that would fit the exact shape of the pebble on the one hand, while, on the other, connecting up with some hypothetical non-existent environment. You can't have a whole piece that is half real!

"For the system to figure out a connecting piece that truly fits the pebble, it has to define the entire shape of that connector—and therefore the next, and the next, and so on. Fact is, folks, it just has to work out exactly the pebble's own shape and you're home! It's like, the more you find out about the pebble's environment, the more you find out about the pebble!

"You see, it's like we said, everything has arrived in its present state in one way only. The energy that makes up the pebble—all the molecules, electrons, forces and polarities—that pattern could only be as it is by having arrived by one particular path, so to speak, whose relationship with its surroundings is itself so intimate as to make any changes in the one show up in the other.

"It's as though the fate of the fairy who left her footprint on the pebble changes the character of that footprint. If her fate, long after, is tragic, that tiny footprint echoes the tragedy in some way. If you have knowledge of her fate, you will see it in the footprint. Conversely if, as Sherlock Holmes, you apply your magnifying glass and careful observation to the small trace, you will realize that there is a fairy weeping further along the shore.

"This is only possible where consciousness is looking at consciousness.

"In short, the system can work out what environment must have arisen for the pebble to be where it is, as it is, at a specific time. This is because it can only have arrived there to become what it is in one characteristic manner. It can only get that way one way! That's the extent of its individuality. There you have it, one pebble.

"Now, if you want to know how I know it's conscious?"

"Possibly," teased Bellarose.

"Maybe!" said John.

Without hesitating, he continued, "Nothing is completely separate, no man is an island, completely cut off from nature—or woman, or from woman . . . anyway, it's a true saying, as it turns out.

"Put another way, when any two things connect, they must at some point truly connect, that is, merge completely. Otherwise they will never honestly, truly, connect at all! Ultimately, you can't just sort of connect! At some place you must connect completely, if you are to connect at all! Think what this means! If I connect with you, if I touch you, even just a little bit, I must somewhere have touched you completely! If I am to touch you at all, it must be somewhere totally complete. It's amazing, the more you consider it! What does it mean to have any complete contact at all? Does that mean we actually physically merge somewhere invisibly in our energy, even though I just feel the pressure of your skin? Well, it does, yes, it's true. We must somewhere merge totally physically to make any physical contact at all. We call this the 'slipstream connection.'

"This gives rise to a continuity, a slipstream around everything, that allows consciousness to flow through all barriers and flood all areas of life, even into matter! The fact is, wherever you have a connection, you have consciousness flowing, you physically just can't keep it out!

"Fact is, folks, if you can't keep it out anywhere, then it *is* everywhere and if it *is* everywhere, then it *is* everything.

"In other words, if we are conscious anywhere at all, then we are conscious everywhere, and all things are, to some extent, twisted or untwisted, conscious!"

They enjoyed seeing him so excited again; it reminded them of the old life they had shared, falling in love before his disappearance.

Bellarose purred: "Wherever you have a contrast, you have a connection? Think of those changing textures—"

She slowly rocked her shoulders, breasts and hips as though she was on the deck of a sailboat, hands billowing slightly the hair, stretching with pleasure.

Her brown eyes got soft and large, her mouth as though it were forming the lips round the root of a sentence, to bring out the sexual seeds and fruit, to make it all possible, heating up that brew, the essence of memory.

"All those changing contrasts . . . a mystery? Think about it, boys! Anyone for a blow job?"

John looked at Jesús, "Are you waking up to this act?"

"The mystery," he replied, "the incredible truth, is that the unique character, the individuality of each separate thing in nature is just so because it can merge completely with its neighbor. If it could not, it could not be different from its neighbor. There's a polarity there—"

"You talk too much!" She leaned forward, put a hand on his shoulder as if to steady it and took him in her arms, rolled him backwards with kisses.

John watched the wave. He caught sight of a slight blue stream in their wake, with a hint of pink, almost unseen.

The other two separated out and flowed round again.

John plucked a blade of grass and held it up to the light so that it became the center of attention. "This blade will tell you about all the others? How do you feed it to your computer?"

"We can photograph it, photographing its crystalline structure is sometimes helpful. The crystals give us a specific asymmetric pattern. The merging will never allow pure symmetry in a crystal; they're in a changing state of balancing, connective polarity, like the edge of a waterfall. Another reason why Jack avoids the term 'crystal' as misleading, impersonal."

"Impersonal?" queried Bellarose.

"Yeah, another way to look at the soul is the shifting polarity of the waterfall; it has cyclical polarity between the chaotic whitewater and the level, symmetrical pond. But it never achieves pure symmetry. Nothing ever does, we've discovered. The pebble is never perfectly round, never in static symmetry, always in motion, with a slipstream, where the circling balance or imbalance of the soul's energy generates your slipstream opening and closing this way and that around the polarity of who you are, your character, connected in nature's slipstreams. A kind of crystal but more of a chakra.

"So, with a kind of photographic timepiece, we can then grow that crystal more quickly; we grow the information into what we at the Project refer to as a 'data crystal.' The whole thing keeps working off its various facets. We've now got to the point where we can feed in a digital photograph of your face, and the system will take it from there. Beyond belief—wouldn't believe it myself if I weren't sitting here now."

They looked at him quizzically.

"Recently, when the photographs of the Project personnel began to pass through the system, things began to fall apart. So, here I am!"

He leaned back on his hands, the large friendly ears level with the supple mountain range of shoulders against the distant hills, and eyed them, mischievously, smiling.

"It just has to look at your face?" said John, grinning back at him.

"It takes the lines and characteristics of your face and sort of works backwards to find the map of your face, the crystalline structure behind the mask and the direction—like a river."

"It looks at him," said Bellarose, "and says to itself, now where's he been!"

"Where's he think he's goin'?" asked John.

"Ah," said the inventor, "it won't predict the future—let's get that straight from the start. Got into a lot of trouble over that one. Everyone wants a prophetic prophet—forget it. I told them they'd have to stay on the slipstream. They still don't believe me." He hesitated as though checking the weather.

"OK, the problem is this: the system takes into account that I'm its *creator*—me!" He made a monkey face.

P—Perth, rune of the unknown.

# 3. Screen-Watchers

BEFORE THE MAIN SCREEN AT THE Glass Farm Light Center, Glastonbury, Somerset, England, Lancelot Camelot wrinkled his nose. He was "on watch."

The long seemingly good-natured patience of the eyebrows arched upwards over the slightly unfocused condescension in the light brown eyes, giving them a changeable darkness, sometimes to bitter blackness.

"Jack!"

"Lance?"

The wrinkled nose turned into a vague cuteness of a smile as he held his breath, as if to disguise the pain. He was training Jack Bridges by means of carefully timed and numbered silences.

Some of these were inflicted like forgiveness after any use of the abbreviated form of the Christian name.

The Camelot was a New Age affectation. If there were Wise Eagles, Sage Prophets and Arthur Avalons, then why not a Lancelot Camelot? "It says the lot!" he would say, leaving the audience in a quandary.

Now, feeling avuncular, he would release the pressure and overlook the other's shortcomings. "Witness this, my boy!"

The Master would not be afraid of airing the electric truth! He arose with grandiose delicacy from his station and ushered JB to a ringside pew.

Jesús was saying, on screen, "When our photographs were fed into the computer, it soon discovered that the slipstream of my life led up to the creation of the system itself and it therefore regards my slipstream as being merged with its own. No one could have foreseen the consequences of those connections. It just made them automatically. We worked on it in a pretty awful atmosphere. You see, I was becoming a Grail."

He looked around quickly, as though Puck might be there. No, he had center stage.

"Now don't jump to conclusions! A Grail is a software term we cooked up for anything that can shorten the time it takes to reach down the slipstream. I guess I never got a chance to explain that very well."

"It's like the pebble," said Bellarose. "If you want to access things closely related to the pebble, you find the pebble and then you're on its waterfront. Everything has its own slipstream. So the pebble would be a Grail to the rest of the life on the waterfront. You wrote some software to help you locate Grails."

"As a matter of fact, yes, we did—"

"So here you are," said John.

Jesús's eyes twinkled as he scraped the heavily clean-shaven shadow of a beard and cocked his head. "You're right," he said quietly, "Bellarose is a Grail; so is Shakespeare. It's all a matter of where you want to go."

☙ ❧

In the Hall of Symmetries, at the Château de Solion, on the Swiss side of Lake Geneva, Jesús's father, Master of the Temple Priory, Secretary General of the United Nations, was also on watch. "Give me a child until the age of eight," the Jesuits echoed in his memory, "and I shall have him for life."

He listened to John's simple deduction of the truth: "So here you are." The long-haired man was reaching the vital conclusion and the ease of the matter brought an expression of aggrieved dignity to the old man's bearing.

"But you're more than just the average Grail, correct?" John added.

The grin on the photographer's face broke the masterly poise, and the screen-watching father had to clear his sinuses to reassert himself.

"You're right again," the son replied. "In fact, it routinely updates its files with my traces before processing virtually any other data of consequence."

"It considers you a part of itself," pursued Bellarose.

"Pretty much—"

"You've become a standard of truth, of actual fact, a channel in giving it direction on the slipstream. And no one can predict just how it handles your traces in any situation, when it handles other data. But it gives you credit. It takes its direction from what you yourself believe to be true. You're like its photographer, you give it alignments. But it's as though your eyes are built into its lens. And it functions like a camera, so you also give it credit for telling the truth. You bank on each other. And it makes you into a camera for others to see things—"

"What?" Jesús stared at John, then at Bellarose.

Jack weighed the tone of Jesús's reflex question and wondered what the system would make of this conversation.

He had assisted the inventor throughout the Project, always ready to help out, especially when it came to the arduous business of finishing a job, discovering a number of time-saving routines. But he took no credit for the invention itself, so he had not dwelt on its origins or its elusive and mysterious inner nature. In fact, he avoided the issue of who should take what responsibility in the process of development.

He quickly remembered that day when the system began to give priority to Jesús's traces in order to continue processing the photographs. They took a while to figure out what was happening technically, but nothing had been the same since.

The thoughts of Jesús, an apprentice of the hierarchy behind Project Light Center, were now being credited with more weight than those of a Grand Master? How did they know the system was giving a true and fair view? Could they believe what they now witnessed on screen?

The Master, Jesús de l'Orient, Sr., cleared his throat again; how could they be sure the damn thing would do as it was told! The Temple's credit was in doubt.

ǀ—Isa, ice.

# 4. The DOG

JESÚS WAS ON HIS FEET, CENTER STAGE. "So there I am, standing in an auditorium; assembled are some of the most influential minds of the age. The personal power of these guys is difficult to exaggerate. You stand next to one of them and you feel, quite simply, that you know nothing and have yet to experience everything, but only if you do your job well.

"There are politicians, scientists, professors, clergy, leaders from many hierarchies and families from specifically chosen parts of the world. Officially, they are all monks, brothers of the Temple, sworn to the Rule of the Order. They have all taken an additional oath of secrecy concerning the system.

"Needless to say, security is rather tight." He shrugged, smiled. "So here I am, a Templar!"

More of the brothers were responding to phone calls and messages from the two Light Centers. They began to arrive at Glass Farm and Solion.

"Do you remember my old company, Slipstream Systems, Inc.?" Jesús continued.

"We were there when you opened the first bank account," said Bellarose, watching him begin to pace back and forth.

"Well, I'm sorry to say, this is what became of it—me, standing before what I have since discovered to be—"

He froze and stared down along the trees, where he knew the Kennebec flowed wide and slow past the small town on the edge of the North Woods. It was not the exposed British landscape where the ancient hedgerows still served as bulwarks against the enemies of nature until the forests recover from the torment of the old world, its over-long history, slow, reluctant to see, like an addict.

Jesús remembered the priest. He had seen him again down in the town. It had been swept from his mind, replaced with the image of a traditional rustic broom of withies, reeds . . . or was it pollards, he had wondered dreamily. He had bought one along the river Brue that runs through Glastonbury, a typical witch's broom, out of the fairy tales, an object of everyday use in the Westcountry.

Puck had asserted, on screen, that it was he who was always stuck with the broom, that the witches were really just trying to make a typical male of him by stealing it all the time and flying off to the covens!

"Typical?" Jesús wondered. "Who was he, Puck, talking about?"

He relaxed and stepped across an invisible threshold to continue with his story, "To be—an inquisition. Basically a court of judges and their advisors, thinly disguised as an informal briefing on how the so-called DOG was coming along.

"DOG—that's an acronym. It means Digital One God. It's supposed to be a joke. They had taken to describing the system as the DOG: 'So, how's your DOG?' 'Been walkin' the DOG?' I'd been getting more of it each week, ever since we went aboard the yacht."

"Yacht?" said John.

"I'm afraid so—more of a floating hotel; even more sickening when you realize it was their way of downplaying the importance of something they intended to get their hands on, whatever the cost.

"Meanwhile, I was supposed to believe that these helpful gentlemen, a few of Dad's friends, had given up some of their precious time and a few dollars of their vast fortunes to gratify a whim and bring along young Jesús for the old man's sake.

"Occasionally they would come aboard. A harmless segment of a dying world, the international old boy network, just giving me a leg up, what!"

"That was before they put the squeeze on."

The other looked thoughtful. "Yeah, I guess so . . .

"So, I trusted my father to take care of the legal framework, since his lawyers were old friends, etc, etc. So how stupid can you get, right?" He looked up, relieved, smiling, but the question remained.

"So, I said to these guys in the auditorium at the Château de Solion: Yes, there's God-consciousness, but it's probably not large or widespread. As I watched their eyes widen with languid outrage I tried to explain that 'God,' as a concept, needn't necessarily have a soul, that the concept itself could suffice and, like the system, might even be conscious in its own right, to some degree, although it wouldn't be substantially aware of what it was doing—it's just that if it weren't conscious at all it wouldn't function at all, one step wouldn't lead to the other, no one would be walking, etc, etc. The worse it got, the worse it got.

"I wound up apologizing, stupidly, begging like the proverbial dog, pathetically. In the end, I had to leave. I walked out amid the thundering silence of their displeasure!" He tried to smile again but covered the failure by itching the shadow of a beard.

Then something tickled him and he wanted to laugh absurdly. "My father was so livid he had to extend a formal invitation to meet him at the club, in London. He would see if anything could be done. I had mishandled my life, he was responsible, etc, etc."

"It was your company, right?" said John.

"Ah, not for long."

"It was all a set-up."

"You might say so—"

"Probably?" teased Bellarose, though proud of the scientist for eschewing absolutes.

John looked away philosophically and caught sight of a black-robed figure pass behind a standing stone. Reaching back to get their attention, he looked around to find Bellarose leaning impulsively onto Jesús, licking and kissing him over and over, while he fended her off with a silly laugh punctuated with a pleasureful shriek.

At the slight touch of John's hand, they collapsed and rolled, giggling. He grabbed Jesús's arm and the latter pulled himself to a sitting position as the couple rolled back, and Bellarose rolled off into the grass, blushing absurdly behind her hands.

When they looked up, there was the priest.

They hesitated, obstinate, tense, as though caught in the act, about to scramble to the defensive.

John recognized the old program of being made to feel this way by nothing more than a certain type of moral presence, casting a palpable vibration against him. He remembered the days when they said, "bad vibes."

He took back his freedom, deflecting the attack by thinking sex. It was his own version of a martial art against the antisocial, using the Chi. It worked, he relaxed. He saw Bellarose join forces, the way she looked at the man, relaxed her shoulders and straightened her back.

Jesús recognized the priest but made no sign, waiting for the other to make the first mistake.

The man in black stood close upon them for a full minute before addressing them, waiting likewise for any sign of weakness. They held their ground in silence, feeling somewhat absurd.

Suddenly, he spoke: "Jesús, your father has sent me. We must ask you to leave this place at once. If you remain, you will be exposed to adverse weather conditions. He, and all of us, only want what is best for your health and the good of your soul. You are compromised, as I'm sure you well know. But that is—be as it may, it will do you great credit to come with me, now, before it is too late." He paused, confident that surrounding nature would enforce his words with silence.

He smiled with routine benevolence. "Do you comprehend?"

The son turned the word "credit" over in his mind, to check the other side of the coin. Yes, they were chasing him; it was to be expected, but how great was their need?

While he became fascinated, engrossed in the power game, Bellarose stood and faced the priest. She felt a distant rage race quietly from the past as though in streamers before grim ranks of children, women and men, tortured, burned and forgotten, heretics arising, as though world-weary but awake for Judgment Day at the blood-red sunrise. "Leave us in peace! Get back, you have no business here, go back, get back and get away from us!"

He went pale. He had not expected to be subject, after all, to nature, in a body, just a male in unisexual robes that drifted slightly in this dangerous breeze next to a female.

With mock humility, he took a step backwards and stumbled on a pebble, stiffened and swung sideways to eyeball Jesús once more. "Is this your answer as well?"

"No doubt—"

"Very well, we do what we can. God help you, my son." He cursed him with a sign of the cross and turned away.

They watched the shoulders lurch like a black box, cutting into the path along the trees, finally to disappear.

Jesús was still listening to her voice. She had spoken with authority. It had resonated as though, even after all these centuries, the Church, all the Churches, shared in the guilt that could never be contained or outdistanced or explained away with another tale of how it had all really happened and how it was all supposed to be, if only people would get their religion right once and for all, get the Church right, make it work as it was meant to work, as Christ would have wanted it.

The way it sounded to his ears, after all these centuries, the Church had, after all, made a mistake, in fact, a scientific error, yet again, even after the lessons of the Renaissance and the Age of Reason, reformations and counter-reformations thrown in notwithstanding, there had been that continuing mistake in judgment: the Church had not been forgiven.

He wondered if anyone had the authority to forgive the Church. Perhaps, now that it had turned out that they were just plain scientifically wrong about the One God, could that same science become a savior? Were they, in fact, yet to be saved? By an inventor? A miracle jock, a Puck?

Not even the Churches that over the centuries had tried to distance themselves from Rome had been able to forgive their own Christian tradition, to absolve it of the murder, rape, consistent oppression, genocide, the horror stories recorded and pounded into the Bible itself.

Change it, yes—but the blood was always on their Christian hands, no matter how hard they washed them or rubbed at that spot. Why? he wondered, listening to her voice on the landscape.

He wondered if it was, perhaps, humanly possible to have so much credit that a man might save such a tradition with the words, "I forgive the Christians and their Churches," and they would, in truth, be absolved. Then Bellarose's words would disperse, that wave would lose them . . . no more waves like that.

He listened to the wave accumulate, instead. He had learned to hear those waves by sensing their freedom. He had recognized it as a chill along the spine, a hole in the center, a hunger, a mystery, a challenge and frustration, the endless frustration of a debtor chased round the earth by creditors hunting him for just two cents.

Just one cent he had; one more penny and he had them, all of them. The world would be his. But just how badly did the creditors want to collect? How much? Two cents worth? It would drive him insane. He cursed the Brotherhood and all families.

Then he looked at his new family. What now? What if they forgave him? What about Puck? Would Shakespeare's pagan gods hand him just one coin? A handout? Charity? He would never take it! Unless it would be guaranteed to make them into just another Church.

But what if he had to take a risk? Could he live with that long enough to forgive them also, absolve them, too, even the gods? For what? Whose story should he tell? Which myth?

He was engrossed once more. It was a maze. Not even the system could figure it out. So, here he was, hesitating to hand out too much.

Still, he had to give something more. Bellarose and John were looking at him that way.

M—Mannaz, humankind, soul.

# 5. The Cybertype

"OK, GUYS, WE'RE FAMILY, RIGHT?—

"Anyway, it's the future. Besides, there's no other way, right? It's what's happening. In more and more places it's just simply a matter of survival. People aren't stupid, they get practical before they starve. Population pressures can only be resolved by having more parents per child in the family.

"And as for the fifty percent of children born of single mothers—in the States, fathers, together in the community without any social stigma in relation to the mother, are taking responsibility for these children who would otherwise be in poverty. It's changing everything; our old beliefs systems no longer apply, and our sense of what is naturally right is coming through. We have multi-parent families replacing single-parent families, and no one's asking a lot of questions about bloodlines. It's breadlines they're concerned about. And this works. It's like technology, telecommunications, totally new and somehow ancient. And the only way to deal with the fallout from vast inequality from the new aristocracy.

"So we'll have to reach deep into out cultural history, into the tales of the temple dancers, way back, beyond belief, just to survive on this planet.

"We must go back to a time of innocence. We need to encourage having more parents in each family. It's better for the kids that way, and it makes for a stronger economic unit, like the Indian tribe takes responsibility. We must love and work increasingly together. That's what I'm thinking, just now.

"So there's something you should know."

He looked into Bellarose's eyes. It was inexplicable, there was no court in session, somehow he wasn't on trial. The priest was gone, she was regaining that peace in nature. His mind was racing.

He looked at John; their eyes met and the sexual polarity reflected him: for an instant he inhabited John's skin. They knew simultaneously. It was a small miracle of untold significance. It made them feel surprisingly natural, animal, ecological, ultimately united, but Jesús felt an added responsibility for the outcome of a new game, where friendship and competition would somehow become friends as well. That was the challenge, he thought, still able to be animal enough to switch skins, to feel soul enough.

He remembered the *soul* and then strayed back to his subject. They were expecting the truth. He saw it as a challenge. He would be the inventor. "You've just met one of my father's inquisitors. I have to apologize. Even though they've renamed themselves, the Congregation for the Doctrine of the Faith—that's their name now and for the New World Order—it's the same old Inquisition, the Holy Office, the ones who instigated, along with the pope and the Frankish king, the Crusade that wiped out, burned, village by village, virtually every man, woman and child from the Pyrenees to the Alps. And that was just the beginning, back in the twelfth century.

"So France was forcibly united in the destruction of its own most liberated people. It's the old story. It cycled back on them in the blood of the French Revolution. It's the repetition in the maze. Again, with the Nazis, they singled out people considered to be heretics, by setting a moral standard of authority. France is divided."

He dropped into a monotone. "The Cathar heresy was simply that Jesus was a man, that he taught people about reincarnation, medicine and so forth. It was so advanced and widespread that the Roman Church was on the verge of obsolescence. The people were wealthy and democratic by comparison with the monarchy in the Frankish North.

"But the Cathari were pacifists; the South had no defense, very little government. France is still struggling with the legacy today, calling on a moral authority to unite it, to justify its military and economic strategy. Now it's the European Union, the U.N. It's a maze, it all comes back on itself, like the concept of karma.

"I'm reminding you of all this, even though you know it already, so you realize that the Church stands on its own tradition. There is no repentance, no forgiveness, and no quarter given.

"The story goes, when Montfort asked the Church how he should tell which ones were the heretics, the answer was given, 'Burn them all! God will know his own!'

"So—people forget, but remember the pebble? Ah!

"Now, in all honesty, if we're going to join together as a family, there are two more things you need to know about what you are getting yourselves into, with me, now that I'm back. I couldn't tell you the whole story. I hope by now you'll understand. I had to find out myself."

She tried to object, but he cut her off.

"I am going to describe to you something that we call the 'cybertype.' The question we should be asking is: how can I speak meaningfully about the soul? It's in juxtaposition to the presence of the cybertype.

"Psychology has made great strides, become powerful, with words like 'ego' and 'archetype,' 'libido,' but, we have to be honest, once again, because the system has shown these names to be just box labels, virtually meaningless, except as a general reference to trigger attitudes and provide a little Victorian history to a truly ancient topic of inquiry.

"What we have to accept is that the hard science has been in the medical profession. When doctors accepted psychology, they were basically endorsing a religion—or at least a cult.

"I suppose a lot of doctors and scientists lose their faith—or they long for one they can't logically leap into. Psychology is just so easy to substitute; it has all sorts of false doorways, hidden assumptions that allow you to build in illusions of science and medicine.

"Anyway, they got away with it because few people have more credibility than a doctor, a priori.

"Also, of course, there is truth in psychology; people sense that something is there. It's just that no one knew what it was. But because of that sense of truth and the credit in the profession, psychology has been able to usurp the reality and overtake the existing religions, threatening obsolescence, as in the twelfth century. But meanwhile it's going mad! No evidence—"

He got a silly look on his face. Then wiped it away with his hand. "The law courts accept a psychologist over a priest any day, all on the strength of medical endorsement, even though there's been little or no substantial evidence for any of it. Still, psychological hypotheses are making law.

"This is the stuff of religion. Even the Church sends its child-molesting priests to the shrink to try to get them accepted back into the community. That carries more weight than the routine of confession and forgiveness . . . Anyway, where was I?

"So, the New Age looks to psychology to get the Churches off the hook and so then it can take all the credit. And believe me, when you look at the power of religion in our culture, the amount of credit going is considerable. There's a lot of psychobabble out there on the docks. Enough to get every pirate out in his ship!

"So, jump overboard and enter the slipstream. Follow a pebble along the beach and into the harbor—what do we find? Freudian people? Egos under the sun? Ids and Jungian archetypes? Libidos galore?

"Now think cyberspace. That's as close to the reality as I can describe what it's like to look into the monitor when you're on the system.

"I can feel you're getting into it now. Yes, there are people there, but—pretend, now, we're on a beach where nude bathing is allowed; that'll make it easier to imagine. Now look more closely: we've all got, virtually all of us, got something on. You can actually see it. You can focus on it.

"Everyone's wearing his or her cybertype."

He shrugged, "Of course, the pirates, the warring monks, the modern-day Templars, according to their collective self-images, don't actually use the word, 'cybertype.' They prefer to call it their panoply, for example. A full wardrobe of armor."

He scratched his chin and looked at them strangely, as though amused from a distance. "Now consider this armor to be the latest in military hardware, state-of-the-art and updated moment by moment to respond to changing conditions in its environment.

"Think of it also as an intensely woven weather system, almost crystallized but still flexible like a net, always pressure sensitive—OK? Add to that a video library of wide emotional content that can deliver replays at the press of a button—the flex of a muscle.

"It can deliver those replays through you, personally. All you do is accept. Nothing more. It's all done for you. You are thrown into the act, you become the part. It feels so good, so right. The path of righteousness is opened unto you. You do nothing. All the energy is given. All your gestures, your body, your words, the sound and resonance of your voice—it's all done for you. The power is potentially boundless, only limited by your credit.

"That's how much you owe on what we call the cybernet. You work your way up a cybercult. You do it with the story, the ritual tales and myths of the cybertype, you can work them up into a miracle, all by not lifting a finger.

"You give the network your soul, and they credit you with a suit of armor that goes on endlessly, a wardrobe, a sliding cupboard where your slipstream is safely enclosed, on and on, boxed and shipped out into the net, harvested for its direct raw energy, the energy of the soul, exchanged.

"That's how we figured out you must have one."

"What do you mean?" asked John.

"What I mean is, you are pure soul, you have no cybertype, both of you are free."

"You mean that you assume that's my soul in action, what's left over on the slipstream, where there's no cyber-thing but still someone's there," said John.

"Merged with the slipstream. On screen, the difference between a soul and its cybertype is not too subtle, believe me! Off screen, it's almost impossible to tell. One reason hardware remains popular."

"Do we believe him?" teased John, resisting his own ongoing internal wars of a combat vet. Talking about being ensnared in an armored net was his saving grace.

"Me? said Jesús. "You want to know about me? I don't know."

Bellarose watched his eyes for a moment. "You're merged with the computer, so it doesn't know either. That's what all the fuss is about."

"They've made you an offer, of course," said John.

"Incredible! How'd you guess?"

"Well, manners maketh man? How could they do otherwise? I mean, they've got to type you somehow, and they want the right responses from the system, all in the service of the One, right?

"Let me see now, you were just bargaining over the cost of the harness when you thought you'd check up on some old friends—"

There was an awkward silence.

"He's already got the computer on his back!" she said.

"Right, I'm sorry. I didn't mean it like that."

"No," said Jesús, "you're both right; it's the truth."

E—Ehwaz, horse, teamwork, harmony, flow.

# 6. Sun and Moon

JOHN CONTINUED, "SO, SLIPSTREAM SYSTEMS WAS going to offer the Holy Grail for sale! At a reasonable price we could own the crystal ball software. Instead of Holy Communion, we would directly access the slipstream, talk with the gods and goddesses. All right! Put us through a few changes. Fortress hierarchies to clean rivers?"

"As long as it's nature on screen," said Bellarose.

Jesús was taken aback, "You mean the gods aren't hierarchical?"

"Puck?" said John, "you must be joking!"

"Listen, I hate to disappoint you, old man; I know what an all-American hippy you've become, but the fact of the matter is somewhat different from what the Founding Fathers believed more than two centuries ago."

"What kind of a line is this!"

"Hey, calm down! It's OK. It's just that it's fairly obvious from the nature of a data crystal that grows hierarchically when we enhance polarity and is inhibited when polarity is neutralized—"

"Sexual polarity?"

"Sure, that's how we discovered that sex is the fundamental polarity in physics. Hey, it would be obvious if scientists had been able to look directly at how widespread sex is in nature, as a force in itself, anyway . . . it's OK."

"So sex builds into hierarchies, it climaxes! You're missing one small point."

"Look, did I ever tell you how we called the data crystal the 'nose'? It could be let loose and it'd run off sniffing all up and down the slipstream riverbank, getting bigger and bigger. More trouble at every turn! Destroyed our self-image at the Project!"

"Getting larger? And back and forth and in and out?"

"As a matter of fact, yes."

"OK, it's the maze, right?"

"Right . . ."

"So where's your hierarchy in that? Where's the importance of your phallic architecture when it's lost in the maze?"

"Well, eventually, the gods started showing up, for one thing."

"And for another?"

"Look, if there's something I've missed in all this—"

"One small point; it's not like you haven't heard it before! If you look at the rock structures along that stream over there, you'll see repeated outcrops of large parallelograms with near right angles, but each one is eroded and weathered in a different way. That's how natural crystalline patterns flow.

"That weathering energy is always there, even if it's the stonemason's, the jeweler's, the diamond cutter's weathering hand. Therefore, the patterns are always different but mathematically predictable by type. That slate will look like that anywhere in the world, but weathered differently in each place, yet with the same worldwide climatic patterns. Where do all the changes and similarities end? There's a rhythm and a music in the stone.

"All stone, all nature, exhibits this silent textured music. It flows like music, and so its hierarchies are just patterns that recur endlessly: the thing is, they are not absolute hierarchies of power! They are not power blocks! There is no pure symmetry to complete and uphold them. Their power is in the infinite stream, in their connected asymmetry, not in being hierarchical crystals, absolute male or female!

"The slipstream's power is always there, subtle, whether the rocks build into castles and kingdoms or not. No one who believes that power ultimately resides in hierarchy understands or appreciates the nature of infinity or the infinite or the Tao, or love between varieties of partners for that matter, or even their own god. It's the politics of nature—fundamentally, asymmetry is inclusive; symmetries would cut you out."

"Yes, I remember you on this one before, and if I didn't know you better, I'd say you were working up one of the old saws on your cybertype. However, unfortunately for me, in this case, the system does have a discipline: it forces me to look at the truth, unless of course—"

"Unless of course its inability to type you has led to serious deficiencies in its ability to focus on the rest of us as well. But you decided to show up anyway."

"Forget it. Listen, we'll all go crazy. This is what I'm warning you about, hanging out with me.

"But not to get sidetracked, let's get back to the Founding Fathers. So what you're really saying is this: The slipstream is the law of nature, as in the Way of the Tao, the Chi, and 'to assume among the powers of the earth, the separate and equal station to which the laws of Nature and of Nature's God entitle them' is—well, missing the *s* on Gods."

"Close as dammit," said John. "I mean they were deists and freemasons and freethinkers and who knows what. But Jefferson knew his philosophers. He wasn't the only one who knew it hadn't been proven that nature is democratic. They had to go with holding these truths to be 'self evident' and hope for the best. Maybe some science one day."

"They did, of course, get a lot of their specific democracy from Native Americans," added Bellarose. "They could see it in action, what was left of it. There are lots of democracies to choose from, and the Ancient Greeks had a time of it reconciling it with their gods, as they worshipped them. Look what happened to Socrates, fer Chrissake. But if the Founders had been Indians, there would have been Founding Women! As for being philosophical slave owners—"

So now what? I should lower the price on the software? It's a bit late."

"It's an ancient science, your crystal ball," she replied, tickling him with her foot.

"*E Pluribus Unum*," commented John. "The brothers ain't happy."

"You can't be separate from your neighbor without making contact with him or her . . . even if that means war!" she added, moving her toes up the line of his thigh.

"We can test that right here and now," said Jesús. Go ahead, feel it!" He raised his hand, as though holding up the sky, palm open, fingers outstretched.

"Feel the tension, check it out, check out the cybernet, it's palpable, yep!"

They kept their hands on the ground.

"It's generated through repetition. If you tell the same old story over and over long enough, you'll actually build tension."

"You're joking," said John, deadpan.

"No, it's true!"

"No, look, I believe you! Go on."

"Well, it's just that those natural patterns, like the rocks over there, even machined patterns within their tolerances, even the atomic clock have leakage . . ." He shrugged self-consciously. "If what you say is true, that tiny inaccuracy spells disaster for the guys who want to corner the slipstream . . . No ultimate hierarchy, after all . . . No perfection, no perfect market square . . . We had it down as a failure of sexual polarity . . . My mistake, I guess.

"The slightest deviation from the ideal of perfection means no ultimate hierarchy, ever. So it all comes crashing down for them when that means—no God! That's because that atomic clock, for example, is measuring infinite time that can't be ultimately separated from the changes that take place everywhere anyway . . . time being physical change. Now, where was I?"

"In the maze," commented Bellarose lazily.

"Ah, of course! So they block the slipstream by repetitive action. Just try to repeat the exact same pattern over and over again, and you end up building blockages against nature. You can dam up the slipstream into reservoirs. A cybertype can then be installed like a mill to transform that energy into more ritual blocks to further empower the cybercult and its mythology. All the cybertypes really do is get off on the same old story, like what you hear from your family all the time, know what I mean? It builds up the pressure into an emotional weather system that is captured in a pattern of crystalline repetitions. Like being trapped in a room with wallpaper that drives you crazy, except that you're addicted to it; you can't live without it! You get a perverse pleasure.

"Meanwhile, all the energy that would have been used otherwise by that boxed-in soul is then freed up to be harvested by more of the structures which, like building blocks, can be used for any number of operations. They can be designed into more cybertypes. They can masquerade as an oracle of nature, anything.

"But there is that programmed feel to it, the sound of the beehive, because behind it all is the constant drum beat, the endless seeming humdrum, the chanting monks and so forth. The usurpation of the slipstream.

"In fact, we've now advanced so far as to discover the most ancient science. Even continuous monotonous silence can be used to good effect to build power. Any ritual to drum up a storm. The cybertype is the most sophisticated version on the face of the planet.

"So, if you feel for it, you can actually tell if it's very intense in the air." He raised his hand again, but no takers.

"So there are two basic cybertypes on offer," he continued.

"Is this the pitch?" asked Bellarose.

"Each falls into three categories of offensive and defensive action, each in turn with their programmed forms, gestures, mannerisms, like a workaday martial art. The Brotherhood has some fancy names for them, but Jack and I just categorize them with the letters A and B with numeric subscripts."

"You let slip something. Their energy comes from blocking and destroying. That's their motive in building anything. Otherwise they would have figured out about the power of the slipstream. Now, that ain't no good effect!"

"OK, evil, if you prefer." He shrugged again, slowly.

"Or how 'bout demons! I'm just an old-fashioned girl! It's the enemy, that's easy enough to see.

"But the whole thing's alive! That's why your system has hurt them. Nature is manifold, many gods who love nature! Demons who hate it.

"We've come a long way to figure out something people have always known. Science has been building a superstition about superstition! Now we're finally getting that old-time information from our technology. The maze is back again. Sometimes you have to go way out on the outer ring in order to return near where you were, close to the center.

"When Jefferson wrote the Declaration of Independence, he was reintroducing the Hellenistic gods. I mean, for goodness sake! They knew it at the time. There'd never been a democracy with just one god. And they knew, along with the issue of slavery, including the issue of women, that one day, in the future, the issues denied would all return.

"In the end, no god at the top of any hierarchy can afford to be protected by a democracy. It won't wash without hypocrisy and corruption.

"As a democracy progresses, it has to face the facts or go into decline, like Rome.

"Any democracy will eventually come under intense fire from a monopolistic religion, let alone merchant monopolies. And for the very reason that the democratic laws will try to protect the freedom of all believers, of all its resident faiths. It reaches a point where it is so successful in protecting them that certain religions will attack, accuse it of becoming pagan; they will see it as the usurper of their God and start up another crusade.

"No monotheistic system can give nature and its egalitarian laws that ultimate credit for ensuring its very existence. Because of that little ole thing called sex.

"That's what it's all about! Isn't that what the system is telling you in generating the data crystal? There is no creation without at least two creators in polarity, male and female, for example?

"That's what's developed into the system, that awareness—you didn't figure on that when you started building it, did you?

"Isn't that what the PLC is downplaying all the time? The big Masonic secret that they keep and lord it over their families and try to bully everyone with it all the time, all those men in their lodges! Creation is manifold! And don't they know it!

"Everywhere creators under sun and moon. I mean it's just basic sex education! But we're so blind to the obvious. We're afraid to tell our children about sex and we're afraid that there are gods who have sex. Basically we're terrified of nature!"

"Why?" asked John.

"Because someone is frightening us."

"Who?"

"Demons."

"Let me just say," said Jesús, "before we get too carried away here, the demons may have some technology, but they have, more than anything, memory.

"In fact, these demons do relatively little planning, as far as we have been able to tell, Jack and I.

"The cybertypes work off of the past, they react mostly to old traditions and operate in a feudal mode, but they seem just as happy in a democratic society as anywhere else. To them, it's just a question of what kind of animal they're fattening up. Their whole life is in relation to whatever the creative soul finds to be of interest. They, of themselves, have little or no life or interest. So they don't have long-term projects, as such. So they don't really amount to a conspiracy.

"They keep endless records and genealogies and stuff like that. They're not what you'd call forward looking. Otherwise, of course, they would have figured out the relatively simple things you've just been reminding me about, infinity and its effects on closed systems and so forth."

"Who are we talking about?" asked John. "Us? People? The armory?"

"Well, in some cases, both. The cybertype is really just an addiction to a mindset. Anyone who has lived with an alcoholic will understand, or a gambler, a drug addict. Unfortunately, an addiction is often just an excuse to attack.

"So, Bellarose, do they realize that nature is manifold and polytheistic? Is this some big secret that they carry around? The question is, even if they did, do they care? No, of course not. Some are so addicted that everything's mingled and merged inside the soul . . . and some . . . well, it's strange . . . like looking at an empty suit of armor . . . extraordinary power, without polarity. Sometimes we'd be working on the system, and the cybernet would start to crowd the screen, like a virus."

"How did you get rid of it," she asked.

"Not too difficult; we'd enhance the sexual polarity of the data crystal. That would eventually clear it from the stage, so we could get on with the show.

"It's just a question of knowing when to release sexual tension, when it builds. It's a question of degree."

"And without a computer . . ." She tickled him once more.

John looked at Jesús. "Here's this guy who figured sex for a weakness because it couldn't build the everlasting hierarchy. Now he knows just when to have it! Don't tell me. This is one big seduction scene, isn't it? Approached scientifically, carried out with relentless logic, backed by proven technology, can't fail! I never saw anything like it."

"By whom?" said Jesús.

"So what was that other point you were going to tell us about?" she continued, prodding him gently.

He took hold of the bare foot and held it. "Ah, there are two kinds of maze. The one blocks and confuses. The other is a natural guide.

"The stones were laid out in mazelike patterns in the landscape. People danced with music and released the slipstream energy stored up in the stones by having sex. It sent out waves. It weakened the cybertypes by strengthening sexual polarity.

"It's useful to remember that a cybertype can have a powerful built-in sex component. It's given as a reward, but it's not a polarity as such, it's just an aspect of the type. It functions as a sexual manipulator, confuses the hell outta people. It's the 'I fuck you, you fuck me,' program.

"The truth is, the entire cybercult functions by neutralizing the ambient polarity on the slipstream; we call it a 'monofier.'

"The players are awarded points of credit that can be given in many forms for contributing to the depolarization of an area or individual. The richer the slipstream of the region or of the soul who is attacked, the greater the credit awarded.

"Ironically, their hierarchies are built up on the sense of randomness you get from constant repetition. It all becomes absurd and pointless, along with a host of other negative impressions.

"But they turn these back on the mark: that's the art that preserves the hierarchy intact.

"Still it has no fundamental direction outside what's going on with its intended victim. A typical approach is delivered with the idea that you've won the pools, just 'cause you're you, you're a winner, so the self-centered ones fall for it first. Nothing new in that.

"We figure stone-age technology is at least as old as the cybertype it was intended to handle. Hence Jack's name for the new hardware: New Stone Age. He was getting a little bit weary when I last saw him at Glass Farm.

"An entire region would come under attack and gradually be characterized by a cybercult until the country was finally overthrown and dominated. But first it would weaken from within.

"Name certain areas around the world, and you'll see what I mean. When I say 'central Maine,' what types come to mind? Things change pretty quickly in the States, but consider the old-world countries. You are typed, often without question, programmed, by your place of birth, race, religion, family status, it never ends. And always somewhere, the feud, the vendetta, where people are enslaved in a storm of false characterizations.

"So some Freemasonry does, in fact, figure it can develop a certain area to become like this or that type of a community. Then they end up having turf wars, of course. Some Freemasonry helped.

"So here I am, basically, caught up in a turf war, over the moral high ground. The difficulty being, once you get into one of these situations, if you lose, you can lose your energy, pretty much go down the drain, like in a hurricane, everything you've got, down to the last drop. But, of course, I'm not sure what that means."

"Well," said John, standing up and stretching, "it means war—and love. You guys had better open up the slipstream."

He was looking toward a Manitou stone, once used to recognize the midsummer sunrise at the head of the vale, in a small field.

"I'm going to check out the ley of the land. I'll let you know. If it feels clear, I'll travel downstream and join in the fun—if there is any." He looked down at them grimly, his eyes twinkling.

Bellarose tossed her hair back with both hands and thrust out her breasts, licked her lips and looked up at the sky.

Jesús, with the sun in his face, looked up at his newfound brother.

John had to smile at that silly expression.

Again, suddenly, they switched skins as though joined in a memory. Just a couple of half-human animals, two mythological creatures rambling about with the nymphs of Arcadia. He'd see him around!

He turned with determination and made for the heel-stone stone. Arcadia was a thin dream on the landscape.

But there were a variety of these markers erected on high ground, even as recently as Shakespeare's day. Some were visible, others were still to be discovered among the trees. Many thousands throughout New England.

"One thing—as a scientist, Jesús," she was sitting in his lap, facing him, her legs, long, soft, extended past his back, her feet playing the grass, "one thing . . ." and she kissed him softly, bending her knees to bring her calves back against his thighs and rise up slightly with her thighs along his ribs, counting them without numbers, "it's this question of doubt . . . hesitation. Is there any basis for it in science, in fact?"

He soaked up the slipstream fountain that gushed from between her breasts, from between her hips. "Do you really want to know?" He looked up at her mouth.

She sat down meaningfully, "Yes I do!"

The inventor proceeded: "Well, even well-established physical laws are repetitive, so far as they predict, so they should go through natural changes. Nature is endlessly creative!" His body was receiving her slipstream in his inner vision. He began to feel her dance in many times and places, moving with black hair, moving with blond hair, red hair, this way and that, pausing to smile at him while he sat in stillness as the stone, in polarity with her in motion on the landscape, coming together in sex. He realized his eyes were closed. He marshaled his thoughts.

"Nothing is completely random, so nor is any one thing once and for all time finally true . . ." He lost track, flexed his muscles.

"Things that are true," waves broke over them, "always dance, they flow . . . they're sensual! Sometimes they appear still, like a rest in music."

As he talked on, she was opening his shirt, covering him in kisses, each one different, until his words became syllables and blended in sex.

Ei—Eihwaz, yew tree connecting life and death,
Yggdrasil, tree of many worlds.

# 7. Temple Dancin'

JOHN HAD SAID HE WOULD COME along down the stream to meet them. He was alive in their love-making, so they had paused long enough to find the water.

It was clear and leech-free, so they had set aside their clothes and stepped in the sun among the glistening pebbles to feel the unconquerable glide round their surfaces and groupings.

Jesús had listened for the moon-language in the water, and they had begun to wash each other. Their laughter had splashed over them with the cool fans of crystals swished upwards and the harmless shattering cascades of liquid light.

It was the day before the fall equinox. The leaves covered their nakedness fleetingly with bright colors. It was hot for Maine at this time of year, encouraging them to enjoy sex. Even so, they had felt somewhat exposed to and endangered by the nameless imprecise morality that still generalizes on anyone who removes his or her clothes.

They had been shrugging this off like an unwanted and over-familiar garment. They fought back with the sleek expansiveness of light and the warm unencumbered air that circulated and awakened their bodies to the oneness of surfaces in the intimate contact between textures. Differences in mind, body and soul melted in touch, in sensual vision, the fantasy come true. Trees were no longer just trees but projected spirit. Rocks, boulders and pebbles had become live gems and reclining love-seats, things to be approached literally nakedly, in the now.

The present had become the past. The truth was again reincarnation. He remembered the way Jack had said, "Nothing communicates between lifetimes like sex. Sex is the carrier wave, the core of the slipstream. It's not just in your balls, Jesús, it's the vision, vision in all ages! What I mean is, the seeds of events flourish and die, but they are remembered in seed form again and again. Those seeds of soul memory have all the volatility of pure consciousness . . . They are potential full-blown memories that can be brought to light by degrees in sex. Or that third-eye vision that comes across sometimes in childhood or sometimes at the end of life . . . I remember just knowing I came from another time; hardly gave it a thought, until . . ."

As this memory flashed through his mind, he felt Jack's presence with Bellarose. He imagined them together, Bellarose and Jack. He allowed the image to turn him on, like a video, although he felt, even now, a strange social obligation, a weird sexual etiquette, call on him to resume the part of the active, jealous male.

The fresh insight through the eyes of his friend revealed her to him all over again. It took him back with a hot longing to a time before you had to be possessive and competitive just to get along, just to look right at every moment!

His self-image began to melt into a fantasy about those days, a memory melting into the present, an entire way of life represented now by Bellarose, Jack, himself.

So he relaxed into the culture and saw spirit stars dance along the inside curves of her hips, intensifying like gentle curling waves, to disappear into an infinity of honey and hot light at the nexus of her clitoris, where the animal fronds rose lush along the mound, and he drank from the chalice with his tongue, drinking the sex from along her thighs and down through her fingertips and hair, her face shining in another part of the same dream, the nipples and ribs, her hips again and again, from his hands holding her to his lips in the tide, his aura to hers, hers to his, united in nature, gently, with all that blended memory of landscapes, released in small flashes of heat and light to shine among their juices in mirages, truth of fantasies past, the way it had always been.

The sensual memory opened up like a goddess stripping away centuries of illusion, but slowly. With the slightest revelation, crescendos multiplied over Bellarose, while she danced before men who admired her with honesty enough to transmit through each touch of her lover the truth that brings fantasy to life, until recognition turns it to memory and trust is released as a story at the tip of a tongue.

Incredible stories, danced with the balancing music and drums, by fountains over stone, incense, murals of the temple dance.

Not the sordid usurpation by the enslavement of females in

temples, but science in mythologies about the moon in its mazes of dance round the sun where without the polarity of her sex there would be no sunrise, no history, no balance, no slipstream, no energy, no light, no love, the incredible obvious truth of the moon igniting the sun moment by moment in the live universe, rhythmic harmonies merged with the goddesses, revealed in the feminine sex of the temple dancers, out of the cosmos, the flowers that embraced the stars and gave birth to the galaxies, in the unforgettable lotus.

Bellarose feels herself dance, feels the close attention like rays of the sun reach out and caress her from each man in the stillness of his arousal, feels for the potentials of the soul in nature and she arches her back, stretches her body between his hands in time to feel herself on that slipstream highway to America, to Atlantis. Where did it go?

A flood of bliss washed over her like the spray from a bow wave onto a hot deck with the instant arousal of being carried along the ocean by cedar and cypress, Scots pine and English oak, the resins inhaled, then swallowed with her lover's semen. Her lips press the remaining pulses from the roots of his life in an upwelling of grasses. He is polarized to the utmost masculinity of his soul in her hands molded with the mouth, through lips and along the tongue with the merging sea and sky while leaves of energy branch out and aerate the streams of their fantasy until she knows she is that woman, that this is her way, her pleasure with a man in love on the ocean.

She could taste that climax beyond her body where she lay by the brook that flowed into the Kennebec on the rung of a maze in time. She felt the bending cycles of the maze resonate through the breaking waves of memory. She sensed its vast increasing harmony awaken in the fields of grass and corn, in the garden among the herbs, the sunflowers she and John had planted together.

The standing stones had been positioned and rearranged, destroyed, removed and re-erected over time into a maze history of their own, reflecting both the consciousness and the ignorance of the people. John had decided to rest against the gentle root of a boulder, polished smooth as glass two thousand three hundred years before.

After a while, he noticed a fine vibratory massage work its way from his inner being to the edges of his physical body.

The quick alternations of energy opened up an alternative body of energy to his will, like opening a book and thumbing through the leaves.

As though stopping at an intuitively chosen page, he lifted his arm in the vibrating field and discovered that the earthen arm had remained in place!

He felt that the book of his entire life history was opening up. It was familiar; he recognized the event like an old friend.

So, although it was the first time in his life this had happened, he remained calm with experience, as though he had rehearsed for the moment. He restrained a strong desire to jump up and run around.

He looked down at the organism, the arm and hand, resting like a specially adapted plant or root in the grass, viewing it almost with the perspective of a naturalist, wondering how it might be classified and what it was for, how it fit into the ecosystem. The impression was fleeting but thrilled him with the implications. What about the rest of him?

He made a comfortable fist in the air, coming to terms with its near transparency combined with no loss of physical pressure. It was still his hand, his arm; it felt the same, but lighter! It existed in an enhanced medium that he had almost forgotten during his current lifetime, even though he had philosophized about it. Now he could feel it in action.

"The three worlds," the words came to him from having heard them spoken softly before he was born. He felt her easy presence like a cool stream attract his attention to the statement until it opened up his memory a bit further.

He remembered living in a time when it was just accepted, "the three worlds." The gods: we spoke with them and felt their presence; sometimes one of us would see them; they even appeared to us and addressed us at a gathering, or we would leave the body to talk with them, or they would enter one of our bodies to speak with us, and of course, we spoke with them in dreams. The animals: we lived alongside them in nature and related to their world, appreciating that it was also partly closed to us in language and thought and in other mysteries, but we could see and touch them, and often they could show us how to be with someone, just be there in nature, without ulterior motive, just being there in companionship, relaxed with love. They represented the opportunity to feel the love of the gods.

The gods and the animals would merge to help guide us in the maze, in the three worlds that we, in our social human world, brought together with them, often representing the gods in animal bodies with human faces, while discovering ourselves: old souls, young souls, some of us having been discovered as so experienced as to be unacceptable as a baby or a child reborn, because too many of us had kept those "Ancient Wise Ones," and "Elders," too much at a distance and worshipped them as heroes and gods, until we finally rejected them outright, whited them out into One—one God.

White if we were white, bearded if we were into beards, African God, Californian God, New England preppie God, Texan gun-slinging God, Southern Bible-thumping God, Jewish God, Muslim God, always God with a qualifier, because we couldn't distance ourselves from the love of the gods while hoping to relate at the same time to the three worlds that have fallen apart in so many ways.

Then came the question: Who had the credit to claim to be the one and only Son?

John trembled as though boulders cascaded downstream.

Alexander was dead. All the records would be destroyed for hundreds of years. One of his generals, Ptolemy, had crafted his own agglomeration of godlike features, Serapis, the god invented by a committee to characterize the New Alexandrian World. This rising philosopher king would interpret for the wild-Western-style Greek colonies that would be Roman, their Mediterranean heritage.

Such power! Alexandria! Ptolemy Soter, crowning himself Pharaoh and Savior, a god by his own law, in betrayal of the Hellenistic Dream.

History and the discipline and dedication of Greek soldiers, had made him the cultural heir to the known world, this Ptolemy, entrusted with the victory over the hated tyrant, Darius. Entrusted with the outcome of all that intense Egyptian history, to bring the three worlds together in nature's democracy once more, from dynasty after dynasty, from Atlantis.

He would speak for the silent statues and symbols, for the Sphinx and from out of the pyramids. Credit to challenge the gods! To claim to speak on their behalf.

All given to him, an average man, a Macedonian, by a technology of warfare in the hands of a man who shared that Hellenistic Dream, a man who helped Aristotle fund the largest collection of democratic constitutions the world had known—but who had died of his wounds, leaving, like others fallen in battle, not a bloodline heir to a throne, but the birth of a federation in trust with the powerful few, and Ptolemy, his half-brother, demanding responsibility for the soul of Egypt and the credit to decree the shape of the a constitution for the freedom of the people from India to the Atlantic.

It was squandered on the fashionable features of the one to be worshipped for the edification of the Greeks, the uplifting of the Egyptians and, at the end of his own dynasty, at the predictable end of the Roman democracy, for the good of Imperial Rome, the god, Serapis, yes, but always Serapis plus— After more than three centuries of Alexandrian hierarchies of cultural pressure, ringing Alexander's name in Roman ears, ad nauseam, Serapis enhanced! In a cynical, vacuous, sadistic Rome.

No longer just a bit of Zeus and some Hercules thrown in, Hermes and the god of medicine, of course, Asclepius, not to mention the keeper of the secrets of reincarnation, Thoth, the monkey-faced scribe, deep in the library of Alexandria with the bull, Apis, with Osiris, the mummy and his wife and sister, Isis, the ever-credited icon of mother and child, give or take a god here, a hero there—but now you have the bearded face of Western civilization, guaranteed by emperors! Finally by Constantine. No more names! Just the One God, One for all—by the grace of our lord, Ptolemy.

The memories continued to open up with new meaning in the word, "veteran."

We should all be so lucky as to inherit the god of the Jews! Having conquered Palestine, Ptolemy and his son gathered those in the Jewish quarter of Alexandria and had the scribes copy out their stories as well, along with those of the Greeks and the Egyptians, the same stories from this point of view, that point of view.

John remembered, he had watched it happen.

Accumulated centuries later, all the Muslims would have to do is react, deny all the mess, all the names, wipe the slate clean! No more symbols, not even art! Just math . . . maybe some architecture, Moorish . . . Indian . . . maybe some names, after all, stories . . . about Jesus, at one remove, off the silver platter. "At least they don't eat him" John mused.

No wonder they named him Christ, the Logos, the Great Connector, the guy who tried to connect it all up, rewire the monster, do the maintenance work on an ageing cybercult.

John opened up his hand and felt the Logos, the Word in motion, never-ending, rediscovered by a couple of computer jocks and renamed, the "slipstream"; why not just call it God!

"Where did that man get the credit?" John wondered. "More Middle Eastern miracles?" All of a sudden everyone knew love?—when they routinely denied it in each other? In Jerusalem? Under Rome?

No way! No—it was him. It was him, again. Ptolemy had returned. And now again, today. Still at it. Still so sincere, still so well-intentioned, still full of promises that he will fix it, still with all that credit and a piece of the latest technology.

"Still with all that credit?" John hesitated, remembered it, the same old story. Why couldn't his Royal Highness just leave it alone! Why always having to tinker with a Victorian monstrosity! To justify himself? Finally to show that he was right all along? When? Where did it begin? And why the obsessive following, the adulation, life after life, as though addicted to his every action: "What will he do next? Is he divorced? What is he doing now? Who is in and who is out? What about his family, do they approve of what he is doing? Why won't the media tell us more! Why can't they give us a balanced report!"

The tabloid wheels of the cybercult, on and on, uninterrupted by life and death, attached to the soul with a guilt of glue and jealousy and apathy relieved by victories, any sweet vindication, orgiastic revelries, over the successful denial of natural realities, over the guilt, the selfishness, on and on, wheels within programmed wheels. All that traction to keep him going, to push and pull him along, die for him. For what!

John felt the bitterness and despair as he remembered the bureaucratic etymology of that one word, God, all the names that had been contributed into its cultural power. And all the souls who had got down on their knees.

This was no Bill of Rights, but a testament to the awesome destructiveness of power blocks. Two thousand years, lost!

But the boulders had cascaded downstream.

He woke up to the present. Like an animal who knows the time of year, he instinctively felt the maze resonate the slipstream. It hadn't rung like that in ten thousand years! Now the years empowered the sound. It was music and thundering rhythms.

It was this life, at last, thank goodness! Not one of those others.

He was in the States. The goddess, like a cool stream in the hot words, Liberty, was quietly with him where they would now stand in three worlds together.

With great caution, realizing with every move, with the lifting out of the other limb, the leaning forward and outward and finally, with the raising of himself up from that body-shaped microclimate, realizing that this could be death in itself, that it was, in fact, death, by degrees, according to the illusions of the age where he arose, never had he felt so alive!

The excitement returned.

Although this newly rediscovered astral body was all but transparent to his vision, being inside of it, he never had any doubt where it was.

He marveled at the fact that he could rub together his thumbs and fingers and touch himself anywhere with the same physical texture and responsiveness of structure and muscularity as he used to have in the earthen body.

It now lay quite still just beyond his slipstream feet.

With concern, but with faith, he leaned over the body. It was breathing and appeared to be asleep.

He watched the chest reliably rise and fall and gave a deep sigh of relief, wonder and expectation.

Then he realized the obvious, "I'm still breathing!

"Am I awake in my dreams? Is this what the out-of-the-body experience is, really? Is this what sleep is, really?"

He took another deep breath. "Wow, but it's in the air! It's the air, but it's . . . it's . . . energy . . . whatever that is! It's . . . just it! It's like everything! It's infused with the whole . . . the whole planet, it all breathes with me, and I'm breathing with it! I'm with nature! I've got tears in my eyes!"

He sighed again deeply with relief. He blew into his hands and felt the breeze from his slipstream lungs and the emotions that flooded that breeze to join the streams of all nature, so completely that his breath was both sent and drawn to his palms, where it curved away in circles. "The weather! This is how it is . . . So, what inspired me to breathe against my palm trees?" Enjoying the play on words, he watched the environment draw his breath along with him, his insight into life other than his own expanding again beyond his body, while his hands began to reflect the emotional release in his breath by coming to life with color.

Golden hues turned pink and spread like cumulus clouds, contrasting as they went with a deepening purple, violet and orange over brown.

Where the colors folded into one another, flecks of white light flashed electrically as handheld beneficent lightning. He laughed and clapped his hands together to make thunder, tears rained from his eyes.

He embarked on a dance round the stone with its lazy earthbound body. The motion of his whirling and jumping and leaping fell naturally into a pattern that was familiar, not entirely of his own design.

He began to realize that he was leaping, turning, stepping to an old jungle beat that had come a long way and had acclimatized itself with fields of corn, with pumpkins and squash, always more squash, brought from the southern Americas to the north and with the history of these transplants brought about, he realized, going up and down and round and round, by the silent musical emotions he was remembering to hear and feel in the weather, as the music of the temple dance panned out in his ears with those sexual patterns building to the blues. Ancient music waking up, feeling good, feeling better, because it *is* going to be all right, if we reflect the lessons of the past, because that's the rhythm of history coming to life, time telling his tales to the moon.

He stopped, looked down at the body at rest. "Never thought you could be so active and so quiet at the same time. Certainly not out of breath around here!

"Let's not get too carried away, don't know how fast you can move on this energy. Things are different, but the farm is still here. How 'bout if I just explore my way down the stream . . ."

With every step, the channels of Chi that looped through his feet into the systems of his astral body unleashed minute pulses, intense groups of waves that had been drawn together, accumulating in his relationship with the sexual polarity of the moon to points of climax in tiny resonating mazes, nuclear chords of music played along his life force, self-propelled with their trails until they release specific memories of bliss in the newfound moment. His feet picked up the sound of the brook. The flexibility of its water carried the music.

From the standing stone he walked climactically to the call of that particular current that overlapped the bank and soaked into the stone where the energy re-accumulated in the crystalline structures until it would curl round the threshold and carry on in the rhythmic beat transmitted by nature's streams, where the heart beats beyond all bodies, in a planetary accord.

It embraced his soul. As he approached, a path of colors caressed his feet like water. They flowed away to a small sugarbush of maples, leaves lush in deep northern green with brilliant red tropical sunsets in progress here and there, hot flowers, stage-lit by birches, posturing columns of light laughing high into their canopies with encoded messages along their feminine sides, live beacons of the musical score. He paused to read from a scroll of birch bark wrapped round the trunk. "The vertical ogham script! The ancient writing, found round the world, on stones mainly. But here we have it! The most commonly found inscription on all continents, goes back over four thousand years."

A vertical line in the white bark connected three straight horizontal marks like weathered calligraphy. "I've heard that word before. Transmits the memory of who we are. Absorbs and releases the Chi—I feel emotions comin' through!

"Killin' trees for paper is *askin'* for trouble. They didn't used to—Only in the last century the boys decided, knowin' stuff like kenaf is better for the job—

"But kenaf, or hemp, or whatever else they had, recycled rags, paper! It ain't no tree! Here we go, look out!—

"Paper from trees has religious impact, goes against the shipbuilders, the clipper ships, the symbols of Liberty, Asherah, symbolized by the tree and the wooden pole in the sanctuaries with Yahweh or Jehovah, before the wood was cut down and burned. Attacks way back, the ships of the ancient Holy Land before it was holy, the shipbuilders of Biblos, before the Bible, the Phoenicians who brought us the alphabet and who wrote the names of their gods the world over, as their name for this one god is written right here, and don't those boys know it now, because that god's initials show up bold as brass on their very own Masonic regalia—Baal!

"Our masters in stone-craft are not blind to the name that appears on standing stones the world over. And they know how nature feels about trees!

"But they'll speak for JB, an' who'll be the wiser? Sshhhh, it's a secret! Power in secrecy! Ssshhh! Quiet, trees! Whisper it! From coast to coast, across the oceans. Ssshhh! Shake those leaves, hear it in the weather.

"There it is: one horizontal line for the letter *B*, the ogham didn't use vowels, followed by the horizontal pair close together for the letter *L*—shakes them Christians outta their trees!

"Come on, boys, everyone's gotta join up!

"What's Daddy do in the lodge? Mom, what's a glass ceiling?

"Who's that JB, anyway? I thought they said he was Just a Bear! Baal, god of the thunder and lightening? Jehovah and a weather god? Together?

"Everyone's gotta join up now!

"I mean, no thinkin' man's gonna take on board those Bible stories without a little work on the mysteries backstage!

"Hell, they gotta know there's someone back there takin' care o' things! So they don't have to work it all out alla the time just for themselves.

"Let the boys with the higher degrees who specialize try an' figure out all those *J*'s and all those *B*'s who've been approached an' been joined up.

" 'Cause, hey, listen, the good guys, they got work to do. There's a democracy to run, an' it don't run by itself. No automatic pilot, understand? This ain't no cyberspace.

"Who's JB? Who cares!

"But, hey, you gotta join up, if you want to do somethin' about helpin' out.

"Ya want to be a cop? You think you can do that job for that kinda pay? You better join up.

"Head of the FBI? Better know who's in the lodges. Every little town across the States has got its churches and round the corner, its lodges. So what's happenin', man! How you gonna know shit, if you ain't one o' the boys? You better be joined up just about everywhere! And you're a woman?

"You think you can do somethin' about all that bad stuff everyone's sayin' is goin' on in politics? Help a whole lot o' people to be free? And maybe they don't believe ya! Have you joined up? Are you, like, 'Ancient and Accepted,' are you *Free*, boy?

"Or maybe you're still a slave! You say you're white? And, no, you ain't Jewish or nothin'?

"So how's your credit in the community these days, anyway? At the bank?

"You? In the property market?

"Feel any small pressures t' join up?

"Haven't you been approached?

"What's that you say? Jericho was Canaanite and they were just Philistines and you meant Phoenicians?

"And you're interested in what about that temple Solomon built for that little ole moon goddess Astarte? And Jehovah is the god who gave Canaan to the Israelites?

"What d'ya mean, what about the U.N.? Twisted the arm of the British Empire to hand over the Holy Land? What's this? Everyone knows God is an Englishman, mahn!

"More hands needed backstage!

"You want to know how anyone with anything serious to do can paper over all the cracks in the masonry. That's what you want to know. And Jericho is over ten thousand years old, already. You're askin' if that's serious work, paperin' over the cracks. Is that a serious question? Don't waste my time!

"We need good cops!

"We need good politicians!

"And anyway, who said good ole Thor's neither an Arab nor a Jew? Or did they figure on approachin' the sun to see if he's got a lightning bolt?

" 'Cause it's gettin' so hot in the lodges that he's gonna have t' be joined up, too!

"Keep that image goin', boys!

"Pressure, pressure, pressure! Call the cook! Where's JB? Take the pressure off! Somebody tell them we're already joined up with nature! We don't need the pressure cooker an' the third degree!"

Emotions of sheet lightning reflected back and forth between the birch and his body, sending coded messages along the stream, as clear as words to their destinations. "I'm a living alarm system standing here!"

The birch trees reflected the sugarbush. He became aware of the maple sugar sap. He remembered tasting the crystals. They caressed his system in the eternal sugar moment, as though a maple sugar maze had retained some of the taste for him now.

It reminded him of Bellarose. The two of them and the kids after school had tapped the trees and boiled down the sap, wondering what had happened to Jesús.

He looked again at the Phoenician symbol of the soul who lived in the weather and guided the ships, whose name appeared in dozens of different forms, even to the name for a local nature spirit, like Puck, but in the ancient world.

In his astral body, John felt his slipstream merge with the weather. "The name, Baal, shows up for thousands of years in the ogham script: The engraving of the ancient Egyptian priest found 8,500 feet up in the Andes in Ecuador, with the name Baal in ogham on his sash and with the tile-shaped squares on the floor, tapered in perspective beneath his feet.

"California! Again, one more footprint inscribed in stone with the name, Baal, nearby.

"Up the Mississippi from the Gulf of Mexico, into the arteries of the States, up the Missouri, into the Rockies, the name is written in ogham along the way, sometimes in reverse, in the Semitic form used by the forefathers of Mohammed, Moses, Abraham—"

John stood by the tree, recalling his history, his struggle to learn, his quest, involved totally in the struggle of others to learn and often to sequester their knowledge to build power over others.

"History should have been fun! To discover is freedom! Instead, all that pressure. Get on with your life! We'll do the thinking outside the box. All you have to know is this, that and the other! You've got your assignment, now get on with it!

"After all that bullshit, who the hell wants to know anything!—"

He became aware that something was pressuring him and that he was fighting back with protective reflexes, like muscles in his aura. "The false darkness tries to manipulate your dreams by pressing from the outside. Psychology that ignores evil weakens the aura. Darkness? What an attack! Collective unconscious? Oedipus Rex enhanced by more shrinks? Speak for yourselves!"

He reached out and touched the tree, reaching out into its electric streams.

His thoughts turned to the Canadian Province of Alberta. He could smell the Milk River delivering its coded syllables to the Provincial Park called Writing on Stone to be absorbed into the natural foundation of the Milk River Monumental Pillar.

He felt the calligraphy. A breeze of mixed energies tickled its leaves, like lovers.

He could hear two thousand years pronounced in the one syllable changing from Bel! to Baal! and back again, until all he could think of was a world of bells calling for freedom from across the centuries, recalled in languages in unison and variation, ringing out and out, reversing and reversing until the Semitic calligraphy engraved in the stone pillar joined the Celtic words engraved in the same stone pillar, advising the passers-by of good and evil and the flights of birds as signs of the weather, signs of the times, syllables migrating back into the Milk River along the sensual polarity of sun and moon.

The prophetic music of the maze cascaded along his hands and arms until he felt the ripples of written words throughout his body, and he chimed with the tree's own music. It sent him away downstream, a bolt of lightning given off by the beacon.

He sensed, catching up with him, the resounding syllables of Baal as they thundered across the inscriptions discovered along the shores of the Great Lakes, the St. Lawrence and into the Gulfstream. The words splashed against his soul from the calendar bowls of Vermont, signaling their incense from the expanding symbols of the Twin Chimney site, incense in water, the meaning in names written in stone, the words say, "For the prosperity of the surrounding land," history rolled into more waves by the word *Baal* with its mysterious extended center radiating like the horn of silence that allows the sweeping waves to break along the seashore, to explode in bliss on sand into foam; from South Woodstock, the Eye of Baal, recorded in stone, guided the ship of John's soul along the effervescent colored pathways of light in the stream, love in times past radiating eternity through the syllables of water from the memories of the sun inscribed in granite crystals, sandstone and quartz, guiding him in his own third eye towards the circle and cross of the Celtic Christian sun-god, speaking from the stones of Peterborough's Petroglyph Park in Ontario, to hand on the craft of the Phoenician builders from untold centuries, back through the Indo-European language groups to Indian Sanskrit roots, before the ships built for Jesus and Mary Magdalene, the Oracle, for the Celts of Glastonbury, for Camelot, before the birch-bark canoes recorded in stone along the Kennebec River, joined by the incomprehensible babbling brook that now brought John into intimate contact with its endless stream of secrets, its gossiping stones of Norumbega, its Algonquian syllables, its Celtic lore, its Egyptian memories and its unquenchable flames of the Fertile Crescent, intermittently enfolded, again, in absolute bliss.

Curved liquid bells of glittering sound now were his ears! Listening to light around glistening stone repeatedly, his ears poured sound down the brook until he roared with laughter through the rapids.

Nature collected him in a small pool at the top of a falls where a mill had once stood.

The water enfolded him with the sexual realization of his human form, and he found himself in the arms of a goddess: Astarte? Ishtar? Asherah? Inanna? Such names! Goddess of the temple dance, a name within a name, now in the shape of a simple water spirit, a nymph, a pixie, no less! As they arose together from the pond, he smelled the incense, the Hellenistic Dream of Babylonia, now the American Dream, the fluid democratic balance between man and woman, man and man, woman and woman, dance in its mysterious equilibrium of love between him and this goddess, arising together from the level pond, arising with the memories of nature.

His soul went out to other men, and he could feel them embrace her in return, or look for her with memories long buried in the heart, struggling to be free. He was united with those she embraced.

In the degrees of sex that are the syllables of the temple dance, in the drums alternating the hues of sound, stone to stone, tree to tree, hilltop to hilltop, the neutralizing anonymity of evil withdrew further and further from the Kennebec River Valley, while the slipstream opened up along the stone thresholds that guided the Atlantic seafarers off the northern currents to the protected anchorages of the Maine Coast, up along the well-worn pathway to the Lakes of Atlantis to the open hand of Michigan, chosen as the symbol of peace under sun and moon, peace in union with the gods, now, once again, in the maze of history, reunion beginning to unfold, long awaited, out across the North Atlantic ley, to the shores of the Westcountry, now unstoppable in its momentum of accumulated time, as the pressures and blockages separating John's old tired world from Astarte's loving touch gave way.

Her hair became Bellarose's hair, her face, neck, shoulders, arms and breasts; John felt his arms round the familiar form of the back and hips, mysteriously familiar, he had felt them that way so many times and wondered at the mystery of a deepening love within love, soul within soul, joined in bliss, in yoga, as it was once understood, the divine love in sex. Still, the goddess was with them!

But who was she with?

He wondered, discovering alignment in the same direction, joined in a shared polarity attracted in so many intimate and fantastic ways in the same direction, his arms were in an earthen body to hold her to him! Jesús's body, in the temple dance with Astarte, Aphrodite, with Jesús filled with love and the love of a brother joining him. John felt hilarious. "Goddamn, if I ain't a Christian!"

Bellarose had become more intimate and universal, fascinatingly free, revealed, flowering in the shared sex with the harmonizing personal slipstreams of friends and lovers, lost in the wheel of incarnation, but not entirely lost to each other wherever love is found.

Jesús began to fantasize she was also with John, giving up some more of his old personal ego and possessive paraphernalia to see her better in the light of the gods, joined in nature's bliss, breathing the divine air of their sexual love, close to the earth.

Bellarose caught the wave and felt the deepening rush of attraction release her out and out into their arms.

She pressed into the waves of pleasure, changing their patterns to allow sex its thresholds along the erect penis, saturated in the pubic hair. They communicated in the degrees of pressure with vast dream symbols where the slipstreams of the gods amplified the pictograms in a sexual language of the closest most intimate truths about us all. The climactic statements were caressed and allowed free expression to redesign themselves in their love embrace to discover the best possible and most direct truth straight from soul to soul, allowing vast truths, incomprehensible far more intimate and complex truths, to be spoken through them into the slipstream arteries of the planet.

Bellarose was just being a temple dancer, bringing her man to a climax, so natural, like she'd always known that was the way, the yoga, unless you wanted children. Her hair seemed darker, along with her skin, all emphasized by the motion of her body, speaking the language of another culture, long gone but remembered in everyday gestures, small movements that she now gathered like a bouquet spread all round them by the stream. They could smell the flowers. The sweat, enriched by the juices lavished on Jesús's tongue smelled like an oil rubbed into the skin of one he had sworn never to forget. Now the oil was spread all over her hips, up to her breasts and drew his erection effortlessly, in the tide, up and back down and upwards over the mound of Venus and the Somerset Levels with her belly button, a symbol of the power of woman to give birth, the center where sex and motherhood come together in the belly dance, the hot woman who is neither virgin nor whore, the terror of the most macho male, up and down and up towards the seed word, into the fields of grain, the Somerset Levels, by Glastonbury Tor.

He felt her Indian touch along his back, her Indian breasts and the uninhibited full length of her back, reminding him of women who went topfree and the men who could relax in the degrees of sex without having to grab one for himself, just relax into true sex and enjoy the view in nature. It was understood, some more, some less, through the eyes of another came the insights of bliss.

Vividly he recalled the very colors of the mosaic by the fountain, the openness, the bowl of fruit. How she had danced in front of them all, how he had danced and danced, how closely she had related to a man here, a man there, he had forgotten their names, but once or twice a face looked at him and smiled, paused in conversation as though forever, with all the love left unsaid because just a word was enough, the gods would say it all and remember it all for them, so there could be peace once again, and they would meet again because of the music in the maze.

So the temple dance provided protection in law and defense against aggression. Many of them were warriors, and the women, like the goddess Inanna, were often skilled in the martial arts, as a companion to the dance. It was all there in an instant, like a fantasy, but the truth of it came home to him as he saw her arch her back and stand up in the nude and reach out and touch the hand of another man, one who gave her an apple.

He climaxed. An apple? The question climaxed through his mind. The scene changed into another climate as he continued to climax as the climate changed and he held onto her as though she were every woman he had ever loved in one.

The worlds came together along the Gulfstream and into the fields of barley by the Tor, where the sun and the moon in an instant wove a word of climactic sex, a pictogram in the grain, complex, specific, stems bent over and turned this way and that, unharmed in harmony, in the polarities of sex, yet another miracle of nature, in the language of the Logos.

H—Hagalaz, hail, projectiles, disruption, awakening.

# 8. The Hall of Symmetries

AT THE SIGHT OF YET ANOTHER message in the fields of grain, Lancelot raised his lip like a limp curtain over the sarcastic chorus line of flashy donkey teeth.

That was enough for Jack. The scientist rose from his pew, took his floppy hat off the hook, slapped the high priest of Glass Farm on the back and went out.

Moments later, past a few ornamental conifers, he stepped up into his allotted trailer. "Over here they call this a caravan, a rectangle of aluminum and plastic with a number on the front," he silently observed.

It stood on cinder blocks like a fallen file cabinet, still full of the ghosts of decisions to be made on which way to turn, how to travel, by what means, in what manner, by what rule, with what behavior in order to locate the stupendous Gates of Eden: decisions, decisions! Building tension in the place of community until the whole stop-gap measure of a caravan is thrown over in a carefully timed tantrum, the wheels and axles propped up over the years in the abject trivialization of the spirit of discovery, the quest abandoned apparently with the best of intentions, while Lancelot appeals to the United Nations for every kind of assistance.

Jack poured himself a tall cola, longing for a root beer float from along an American roadside. From the old world refrigerator, he brought forth a couple of treasures of ice and listened to the sound of a thousand advertisements as they fizzed, sparkled and chimed within the raised glass, streaming the music of Americana into his throat, quenching his thirst in spite of all the clichés. He set the glass down and stared at it, thinking vaguely, "One of the great international symbols of something—it!" Which reminded him of his task.

He had remained at the so-called craft center with Lance just long enough to witness all three lovers leave their bodies. Then the system had followed the slipstream waves of that word into a field of barley by the Tor, just outside the New Age center where he and Jesús had been stationed by the PLC.

As soon as he saw the symbolic design in the field, it was clear to him that the system had carried out a choice. It could have remained with the triangle of Bellarose, Jesús and John, visible in their astral bodies on screen, but it had moved off instantaneously to where that word was as quickly woven in Glass Farm's token field. He didn't need the sight of Lance's over-accepting grin to recognize the statement inside that word in the grain: "We are here, in nature."

He had caught sight of a female figure disappearing from the triangle. "Well, some people call them 'crop circles,' but they're crop symbols to me. Besides, there's more than just circles; you can't ignore the direction of all those lines and the obvious polarity, like they danced round a maypole or something, like the stems stretch out into the grain along living ribbons of invisible energy, consciousness that just keeps on going, bent over in whirls, clockwise, counterclockwise, straight out from the center, variations upon variations, organized, even in layers, into the hills and valleys. And in the rape-plant fields, no human can bend those stems like that without breaking them, but the gods do it all right, by changing round the crystals in the stems somehow. Yes, dammit, the gods! Who am I arguing with, anyway?" He was now thinking out loud.

The system was considered by the Project to be difficult to manage. The Temple demanded the certainty of true believers.

So credit was the name of the game in running the software. Jack was trying to accept it now, once and for all. "Credit, credit, credit—why?" he muttered. "Come on guys, this is supposed to be science! Where do we go from here, after we've thrown out the working hypothesis? No questions, no go—

"Three lovers leave their bodies. Is that power? Is it death?

"Certainty is credit . . . Therefore make certain they're dead, right? Is that it? Is that how it goes down in the Hall of Symmetries?" he called out.

He had his working hypothesis. But he couldn't get round the fact that he, too, just wanted to be sure. He and Jesús had discovered how the symbols in the fields enraged the Brotherhood to the point of silence. The deliberate introduction of any crop symbol into the computer had to be sanctioned by the hierarchy. It had happened only once. The result was an ongoing backup of tension in the Temple itself.

Now, yet another challenge had been made. This year alone there would be over one thousand symbols: intelligent statements of natural fact. That much was clear; facts perceived as challenges. The system kept picking up on them unexpectedly.

The symbols could be found, long weathered, on standing stones. Many modern-day British towns and cities, in the days of Alfred the Great had been founded on the alignments of the crop symbols. The system had revealed them being celebrated as open-air temples, out in nature around the maypole in Camelot where bare-breasted dancers have since been covered up by the monks and historians who described the scene as a Dark Age.

Alfred had advanced the cause of Camelot. He had helped establish the first guilds to enhance equal opportunity, bringing the round table back to the communities. Temple libraries retroactively weighed him down with the credit of being one of their own. The slipstream system was supposed to function as the extension of that library, with all the right passwords.

But now the symbols were back, more words written in the landscape. So many books to be rewritten to reorganize the accounts. It was the challenge that kept returning; to be met with the alternating silence and rage.

Jack and Jesús had uncovered the most jealously guarded secret inside the Temple: the love triangle. The sensual balance between three, given the conditions of the age, the type of society, the immediate pressures, was a matter of degree: a degree of flirtation, of sex, one way or the other resonated, harmonized the triangle, opening the door to the love of the gods.

Love triangles that were flexible, polyamorous, whose receptive angles were rays of light, not rigid and careless of others, but where unselfish love could generate a flow of energy in the three worlds, these were rare, an art, practiced by all souls in their dreams, targeted by the enemies of nature, especially when practiced awake, with awareness.

The stronger the triangle, the more it balanced out into four, like a bow drawn with its arrow. The opening out of the love triangle into the love of two couples combined could naturally develop an axis of power, grounded like the pyramid on a love square, but one where the energy was released in sex, a flexible love square that could take many shapes, a pyramid of energy re-accumulating and released in harmony with the sun and moon's dance: this was the greatest perceived threat, the heaviest challenge in the eyes of the enemy, the most accurate flight of the arrow along the slipstream, from Cupid's bow, the spear of Athena. Jack wondered who he had seen fly into the formation of that word. Who else had joined the dance?

"Who's the enemy?" he wondered.

Would the power develop among couples along the slipstream in the infinitesimal degrees of their relationships, into their dreams, bringing more couples together who might otherwise have missed each other in the rigidity of accepted social behavior with its innumerable threats small and large?

Would there be a wave of consciousness awakening the world to nature and the love of the gods in the rediscovery of the love between man and woman, the love in the true sexual polarity of the soul itself, many times over while the three worlds merge? Wasn't this, in fact, what was already happening, while liberating same-sex personalities, in the many polarities of the maze?

"A crystal in the wild. It wakes up in such widespread detail as to change structures in the stems of grain, spelling out the signatures of the gods in the landscape. To the Brotherhood, a rampant computer virus, attacking the data crystal, building tension in the hierarchies.

"Will the lovers reenter their bodies? What am I supposed to do? What does everyone expect, an act?"

It occurred to him, the more he contemplated the new symbol in the grain, that the sacrifice of a love triangle might be seen as a final solution to the internal build-up of tension among the brothers, in the fraternity. "Reverse the damage of the last symbol—get the system back in harness.

"By what authority and what ritual would they get the moral credit from the death of the three in Maine?

"Simply by having pulled the wool over nature's eyes?

"Then again, that love triangle looks a lot like bait . . . Maybe the Temple would fall for it? Would the extra tension from that kind of a miscalculation blow them away? What is nature's power, anyway?

"Me in the middle, acting out a part of some kind? Like this is a preset scenario, and I'm expected to behave one way by one side and another way by another, and if I don't conform to the ritual, then I blow it one way or another, right? Good working hypothesis?"

His mind was beginning to wheel as the possibilities mixed into each other.

"Don't panic!" he shouted.

Jack flopped down into his easy chair, opened a wooden box and switched on the computer. It was completely self-contained with its own data crystal. Not as large as the main system, but adequate and capable of development, with time, in many directions along the slipstream.

He observed the paint, an entire pallet's worth, aged with drips and smears from holding up painted landscapes in the open air, every color of Britain blended with cleaning and care until it was one day varnished over and given to Jack and Jesús by the artist who had finally bought himself a new easel.

It was perfect for installing the hardware and it seemed to give them some comfort of security against the probing screen-watchers.

Jack got up, locked the entrance to the caravan and drew the curtains. He returned to his chair by the table with the case on top, the screen lit up inside the open lid, as though it looked at him with the words:

Welcome to the slipstream!
You are now at the back door of Slipstream Systems, Plc.
Should they set the DOG on you, this door will automatically shut down and become invisible to them.
Go ahead and choose your threshold!

He hoped it was true. If not, then the back door would be identified before shutting down, if any brothers decided to check up on him, assuming they had the power.

He reconsidered it all as just so much theater. Part of an ongoing ritual that simply included the love triangle in Maine.

"This obsession with Shakespeare! It's no better than the crop symbol enigma. The Bard fixed their wagons so good they're still trying to rewire their cybertypes to look real to this very day. Meanwhile his language is getting a little dusty.

"Of course, if they manage not to short-circuit themselves, they might just pick up enough credit off the networks to take back the system.

"They put on the show and everyone believes them. The crop

symbols just return to being, how did Titania put it? 'Quaint mazes in the wanton green?' They'd discredit her with her own words. Old expressions crumbling into instant flakes! Same way they stuff the words of the characters into the mouth of the playwright. Imagine Shakespeare sympathizing with Macbeth: 'Yes, old boy, we just strut and fret our stuff upon the stage and are no more. Good job well done!'

"All those updated Macbeths out there still struggling, four hundred years later, to get out of being identified through their armor! Theater of war! What am I doing here?—still muttering to myself.

"Chanting monks, at it again, twenty-four hours a day, except that they've extended the service into a panoramic enactment of ritual that reaches into everyday life! Hypothesize! Philosophize! Prophets, listen up!

"This is the process of having to work on a system that is supposed to be cocooned in the cybernet, one day to open up the enlightened vision of the All-in-All to the benighted masses under the guidance of priestly software monks. Is it true? Has it got me thinking in ways that would be considered insane by anyone who casually stumbled into the system, along with their cyberbaggage? Well?—"

He thought of Lawrence Conrad. An artist who could fall in love with the South Downs until his brush would stroke a goddess who in turn enlivened the colors with the incomparably smooth curve of breast or thigh, hip or cleavage, while the rivers reflect the light into forests and the moon or the sun reveals exactly where the viewer has always longed to be.

This mixture of sex and landscape, introducing the edges of villages, towns and motorways, it disturbed, in ways Lawrence failed to understand, the conventional eye. A kind of fear of infringement would glaze the eyes of a highly polished citizen who came across one of these paintings in a restaurant or a small importunate gallery.

"An artist popular with those who should know nothing!" quoted one amused headline from Chelsea, where the writer went on to explain that: "The above was recently let slip by the stiff upper lip of that critic, unmasked after a lifetime in disguise behind avant-garde."

The unselfconscious style, making a succulent statement of the obvious fact that there is sex in nature and setting everyday life into a natural environment, introducing our dreams as unpolluted in their ideals, quietly enraged some in a long-term manner.

Meanwhile this artist reawakened in others the memory of a true possibility for the future, or even the present, in the next frolic in the countryside, in the next holiday along the river, or the coastline, where mythology might, after all, be true.

This magic brush developed the longing and the realization that comes with falling in love—and the folly, like over-acceptance and denial. These all became so real to Jack after Lawrence had introduced him to Julie.

The three of them just exploded apart, shattering out of Glass Farm in two or three directions, still looking for the pieces, as far as Jack could tell, still in shock after kissing the summertime goodbye. "What kind of a ritual was that?" he asked himself, yet again.

Even so, the whole thing now seemed so programmed, the way they had acted towards each other, like they were caught up in a machine and couldn't break out of the emotions, just watching in isolation, as they went through all that ridiculous, diabolical weather. He was still exhausted. "How stupid to have shed tears over it!" He thought one more time. "It was all so empty, except of course for the love. It must have been there; it was the only simple thing about it."

He spoke into the microphone: "Bellarose."

It was enough. The system produced a framed photograph, saved off the slipstream. The Bellarose data crystal had been grown and applied as a Grail threshold.

He had the option of letting the information continue to grow by itself or he could direct the system's nose along specific slipstream arteries and capillaries to seek out objectives, if it would comply. He added, "Please locate."

He was never sure who he was ultimately communicating with. All he knew was that the reach of the slipstream connected him intimately with life beyond his comprehension. He tended therefore to be civil.

Then he recalled with disgust the ornately inscribed marble slab above the doorway to the data center in the square tower, called The Crow's Nest Light Center, at the Château de Solion: "There are more things in heaven and earth, Horatio."

"Why can't anyone see through Hamlet, the condescending little bastard! Everyone around here seems to take him for a goddamn hero!" His teeth were clenched. "A little demon bent on vengeance, more likely . . . another fucking aristocrat having a go at the crown of Denmark, more likely; a novel way of going about it, trying to act nuts . . . just didn't work out for the little fucker!

"Just because you've been given a high-class education doesn't mean you haven't swiped your fine philosophical ramblings from someone else, shit! All the more likely!

"Shit, I'd better relax or I'll end up like Rosencrantz or Guildenstern: one more Rosicrucian keelhauled by the guild over the stern, by invitation, RSVP, guests of the grand master himself!

"What's this?"

The system shut down. The screen went dark.

His hands were trembling with adrenalin; he waited a long minute and turned it back on, wondering what had come over him. "Who the hell am I arguing with?

"I never get used to the decisiveness of these machines. After all these years, it can still send a shock right through ya!

"I really gotta take it easy here. Everyone's obviously watching Bellarose, and I guess the system figures it's too hot to join the crowd. The door slammed before they noticed me, good. I hope. It's supposed to let me know if the game's up."

He glanced at the door of the caravan in the dimly lit room. "Guess I'd just pack a few things, get in the car and head out. But before we retreat, time to go on the offensive!

"So maybe it's all just some gigantic ritual, and I'm just playing my part unconsciously, so be it! But maybe they're killing my friends, and I'm getting outta line. Only one way to find out." He looked into the screen, "Solion, please."

The sound of his own voice seemed overly smooth and commanding, as though it were being channeled back into his ears, to keep him from waking up to something. "Who would be watching the castle and why? Goddamn paranoid trip! Russian dolls within Russian dolls, except each one is an entire theater. Trojan horses within Trojan horses with Trojans inside delivered by Romans to Greeks! Thousands of years of Troys and which one's the shinning city? Keep haulin' those boxes, Virgil, truckin' on down the line. Whoah boy!"

The postcard photo of the château showed up in its usual frame smothered by one of the software brothers in vines and acanthus leaves. "Looks like they still give the impression they control the system. So what's in a frame?

"Well, assuming they know I've got this access, then this art-box is just so much bait.

"But bait for what? Who am I?

"Obviously, they wouldn't leave me alone here if they thought I could cause any trouble with this thing.

"Who knows, the system might even reassure me, on their behalf—that I was safe at the back door . . .

"Of course, Jesús programmed it here; he's kinda in tight with this thing lately. Sooo, it's just not going to let on about . . . whatever I'm doing here. I guess I'm looking out for him . . .

"Then again, there's Baphomet, sorta like Hamlet's old man. What does a demon see?"

He checked his watch. "An early supper in Geneva?" Trying to relax, he raised his voice once more: "Locate the Hall of Symmetries."

The mystery of the way the system accumulated the image on screen always attracted his close attention. The slipstream connections that collected all the associated information leading to the objective functioned in unexpected ways; the growth of the data crystal could be unpredictable, although the balance of the sun-moon polarity ensured that it was never random.

While the screen image dissolved, Jack reflected on how the absence of absolute neutrality had led to the discovery that nothing was truly random in nature. All probabilities amounted to approximations, just a lack of information. Flipping a coin had been given a whole new twist of the infinite.

It occurred to him that it might be more logical somehow just to follow the wave that had recently formed the crop symbol. "Just continue to grow the grain? See where it goes from the pattern in the field?"

He challenged himself about still following the Rule of the Order and therefore the prohibition against pursuing these phenomena: where did he stand now, anyway? He tried to relax with these questions, just to feel the philosopher, heading out on his own. Then he snapped back to the moment as the screen presented him with a 3-D image of a box, alone.

The box was breathing, pulsating, percussing silently, twisting slightly as if, luridly, to show off its sides. There exuded a disgusting quaintness about it, unaccountably, even a lasciviousness as it squatted and bulged, revealing itself with sarcastic cuteness, empty irony.

It felt like the opposite of something he had long forgotten; it knew and remembered where he did not. It pressured him with its nebulous files. He wanted to reject its importance.

"After all, it's just a box, a cube." But he was already totally involved.

Other boxes began to collect and connect themselves to it, on the strength of his denial and the illusions that clung to the denial, trivial as it might seem, still engrossed as they were in their absurd little dance, all pulsating in unison like the cells of a group mind.

Then he realized: "Cybercult panoply. The system seems to have taken hold of the net itself and is working back through the armor, back into the hierarchy to get at the room in the castle. While the ritual reaches out!"

The dancing cubes with their little warped sides crowded the screen and diminished in size as the system showed them in their ranks like an armed multitude, rhythmically heaving with the tension of repetition. The stereo speakers began to emit a low hum like the sound of the beehive, but more mechanical.

"Satanic mills!" He turned the sound off.

Helplessly his skin began to crawl with the idea of such inhuman numbers. It seemed to be too late to wake up to the reality; it already had the jump on him and he struggled.

He tried to relax so as not to exacerbate the attack. But there was a void where he needed a weapon; they were using his own weakness, a weakness of not being able to locate where he was weak!

He wanted to panic and just be a box, to join, to close ranks and be in that oath he had sworn to the Temple, repeat it like a mantra.

He wondered if he was looking into his own panoply, an accretion of false attitudes connecting him to the cult, a cocktail of cybertypes usurping whatever he had forgotten: his soul, in a box.

One long year he had been working at the system, long enough to consider it. It cloyed him, hurt him like a lover to think of it. He thought of Julie and Lawrence and his own behavior. He thought of Tanya. He felt his jealousy and possessiveness. These rages had crept out of nowhere and went nowhere. Something was allowing him to see himself more clearly. He felt the wave carry him into the attack, while blowing his own cover from his eyes.

He looked at the boxes, now reduced to a dark background that swarmed and throbbed in an emerging storm cloud.

"Thor? Baal? No way! And no way ole JB's way! Life goes on. The oath is in the ritual and the ritual is in the cult and the cult is in nature, attached there, boxing me in!

"But the connection goes on with every move I make, every gesture, every breath. The oath continues with me, it changes, with me, I'm alive, there is love in me, I have a soul, it can't be denied! It continues beyond the box . . ."

He saw his covenant with the whole phony Temple Project as nothing but an emptiness, a falsehood blocking his love, sucking his energy, polluting nature like particles in the air. "It's a void! Deal's off!"

Beneath the thunderhead emerged another multitude chanting round a recumbent stone where a priest had just torn out the heart of a human sacrifice. He held it high, and the masses burst into joyous relief. The horrible tension of their uniformity had been ruptured with the torn breast of the victim. They could now explode into raptures, still together, still as one people, programmed like the dancing boxes, now that one of them had burst and had its heart ripped out, ripped out, one for all!

In their delirium, it seemed as though the act was purely random, that it could have been any one of them and that they were at one with their savior. A Savior! He had become the focus of all the long tension of their opposition to nature's sexuality; all the long humdrumming of their social conformity had joyously been released in his sacrificed body and blood. They would eat it. Mix it with their food and eat it some more, extending it in ritual.

They would be bound together in him; they could then go forth renewed and absolved in the anonymity of their guilt, the guilt of having just murdered one of their own.

Now, they would continue to abide by the rules and the laws, abiding with their own small sacrifices and exceptions along the way.

Each and every sacrifice would be owed; each would pay. Until that day when, in the random payback society, the jackpot would be delivered and the choice of victim would become yours, handed down to you by the hierarchy of the priesthood and the ruling families, guaranteed.

One day, you would be lifted up into their ranks, or even better, you would be the Chosen, the Sacrifice, the One and the Only, to be raptured away! Guaranteed delivery. Every one a winner.

One day soon: the time was always at hand. Never too late to wash away the sins of the world and be saved now, now and for all eternity!

Tomorrow could be your day. Order now, place your bets! Don't risk leaving it too late. It might be happening to you right this minute, right now, after all!

Now is it! Now! Now you are alive and the knife goes in, the hand goes in and the heart is ripped out! Your sacred heart.

The god of the sacrifice, the king and the people were at one. They rejoiced, they danced beneath the box-laden sky.

Jack felt the stab in his chest. He brought up his right hand to feel the area toward the bottom of the left rib cage. It was like a deep bruise, even into the bone. But the heart was still beating.

He recognized the Symmetry of Sacrifice for what it was: just a program. But he had to face up to the fact that a programmed cybernet could kill him outright, especially if he had a large account and received its protection. It would kill him with his own armor, crush him, drain his energy away.

Death was usually in the form of a stroke or heart attack. Sometimes a slightly more complex situation called for an accident; the emotional patterns emitted could drive the victim to suicide or to commit other fatal errors in judgment, in loss of perspective, the inability to see the larger picture, the loss of sensual polarity, of moral compass.

"Out of line, JB! In more ways than one."

The scene of the sacrifice dropped back in perspective among hills and the valley of a time long past, while to the left, a vertical blood-red wooden beam encroached.

As the system filled in the details, he realized he was looking at a mural.

He beheld the cross of Roman crucifixion with the body of the victim hanging in death, the spear in the side, but the heart had been torn from the breast and laid upon a silver platter, on a standing stone, the bleeding heart, of any victim, any sacrifice at all.

A chalice, supposed to be the Holy Grail, welled upward with blood which overflowed down the stone like a slow fountain and joined the stream that already descended the beam, collecting at the base of the mural with more streams of blood from the historical landscape.

Jack recognized the rungs of the maze where the blood ran down over terraces to mix with waterfalls from one age to the next.

He massaged the bruise in his chest while he considered the passage of time from the point of view of the Temple.

Dominating the terrace behind the cross was the god, Serapis, upon his throne with the sacrificed body of Osiris in pieces mixing with the blood of a sacrificed bull about to be placed in a tomb nearby, whence he is ritually resurrected each year, to be as you see him: Serapis on the throne. Isis, the mother, impregnated without sex, the divine infant pharaoh cradled in her arms, poses in the cycle, while a baboon sits with his nose in a book of secrets.

Stepping down sideways into two more terraces below and in front of the cross, rides a typical Sir Lancelot on horseback, in his Templar robe of the red cross on white. His twin is with him, "two poor brothers on horseback," the Beauséant, symbol of the Order.

Docked in the blood, as though to meet two gods on the great steed stepping down to the sea, the Santa Maria's white sails show off another blood-red cross, while a heretic burns and Indians are brought ashore in chains.

Reeling with the horrors of the Holy Blood of the Templars, Jack stared blankly into the face on the cross. As he focused on its expression, he realized it was his friend.

He looked once more at the faces of the knights: they, too, looked back at him, eyes glazed, with the same face as his friend. "Three faces of Jesús? A father's love?" he wondered. "So, which one of the twins on the horse ended up on the cross?"

The entire painting looked like a dramatized Glastonbury Tor with five levels, including the distant summit under the storm clouds. "Incredible! Who the hell painted that?"

In response to his thought, the system followed the trail of blood as it spilled through time and space to gather into a channel of red tile along the white marble floor.

He looked round the caravan. "Thick as a brick in here! So who's on the menu, anyway!" He felt the cybernet tightening up.

The system followed the tiles to a throne at the center of a red cross that bloomed into a dais in the shape of a rose. A woman was seated there.

"The sibyl," he muttered, continuing like a Hail Mary, "Five sibyls along the Sistine Chapel ceiling showing the way to the altar of sacrifice, sibyls of the Temple of Cybele on the Vatican Hill, before God took the high ground, sibyls in the Temple of Jupiter on the Capitoline Hill, and sibyls in the lodges, sibyls at the College of Cardinals, again under the Sistine Chapel ceiling! Goddamn, and lookie here." On either side of her, there was a monitor with the traditional skull of Baphomet looking out from the cybercult, while she spoke with the demon's voice.

Jack realized he had the sound off. He was about to switch it back on when the system continued along the opposite arm of the cross in the direction of the mural on the opposite wall, passing over the head of the channel. He felt a corresponding rage leap in the confining atmosphere of the caravan. The system was slipping from their control, yet again.

Suddenly he realized he was supposed to be back with Lance at the Craft Center. He was guilty. He took a deep breath, remembering the long-haired man, John, who had climbed to the heel stone as though responding intuitively to a threat.

Jack understood now that he had foiled the avuncular pleasure in having him there to witness a man's death, with the death of Bellarose, to watch them struggle to return to their bodies, while Lance would have surveyed his apprentice for any small failures to live up to the full thrill of the victory, the appreciation of the power of the Project, unspoken, of course.

Anything Jack may have said would have been taken into account in the measure of their control over the scientist. Any small "indications," as they were referred to. All the dragon scales, the plates of armor, should be discreetly in place, like a well-tailored suit.

He marveled with relief at the way his sense suddenly to leave the Craft Center had fallen into place. "Who inspired that one? Titania? Puck?"

He felt the rage surge once again, in the trailer, almost to the point of recruiting him back, turning him against himself and bringing back the guilt, not of being a brother, but the other way round. "I'm so fucking hung up! No, I'm outta line . . . online! Let's keep it that way. They want to concentrate on the state of Maine? They gotta deal . . . deal with Jack Bridges along the way.

"If this little ole art-box is the bait, let's find out now who's gonna get hooked here. As for me, I've been hooked long enough! Fuckin' addicted!" He called out, "Wait!"

The system stopped on a red tile, and he turned up the sound. He heard someone rise from his chair. All went silent.

There were footsteps, then the voice: "The body of our Lord, Jesus Christ . . ."

Silence. Footsteps. Again, the same voice: "The body of our Lord, Jesus Christ . . ."

Staring at the red square, he recalled his own initiation into the Order. It had all seemed theoretical, an occult science, an interesting means of employment for a youthful questing engineer. But now, as he watched, the red stone was him, science under the heel of religion. It reflected his image invisibly, as though it only had to know him and he was contained within its walls like a number, but even more insidiously, a number that summed up his entire personality and revealed it now as just a flat square of blood-red stone, as though to say, "Here you have been sacrificed—it is already done."

The footsteps, the voice, "The body of our Lord, Jesus Christ . . ." The name sounded anonymous, as though it could have been anyone, was meant to be anyone! Now him, reduced to a perfect piece of geometry.

He felt as though the stone would crack and bleed out of line across the marble floor, into the caravan going nowhere. It danced inanely in his pressured vision, although it remained steady on screen. He feared the screen would erupt. He pushed the art-box meditatively back a few inches.

The pressure seemed to ease slightly. Then the symmetries flashed into his mind. He had had to memorize them as part of his initiation. Now they were reversed against him: it was no longer possible to pretend. It was not a quaint board game come to life, full of pageantry, heraldry, and history. Accordingly, he understood them now the right way round: "To the east, the Symmetry of Sacrifice; to the west, the Symmetry of Terror; to the north, the Symmetry of Rule; to the south, the Symmetry of Obedience. That's the way they have it. I wonder how the other three murals portray it."

A smooth, black shoe came down on him in the red stone. It rested there.

He heard the quiet drinking of the blood and the mastication, the swallowing in satisfaction.

It had to be human blood and a human heart, he accepted the truth at last. The system had shown him many times before. The Temple wanted him to see and build up the addiction.

He cursed his denials. "They have to make it real! It's got to be real at the top. The hierarchy have got to preserve the tradition or the people will stray. They can't control the congregation with a theory!

Somewhere it has got to be for real, so it can have its impact on the types. This is science! What am I doing! They live for the day when it will be back out in the open, the day of triumph over nature. Victory absolute. Well, good enough for an old-fashioned family outdoor Sunday sacrifice, anyway."

He was about to smile with relief in his new understanding when the stab in his chest came again, then a knife in the back, another in the side of the neck. Something took hold of his diaphragm, as though his nervous system interrupted his muscles and his breath was halted. The grip slipped, and he breathed once more, slowly, deliberately. He took another deep breath.

The shoe remained pressing down over the stone tile. The two connecting squares bled systematically off screen. The voice had stopped, while they waited at the crescent-shaped table, before the sibyl, waited and weighed on him, usurping time.

"Wise up . . ." The syllables fell through his thoughts, as he slumped against the table. "Obvious! So they're finished with me now . . . I die . . . Obvious, dealing me out of my body. No more energy . . ."

But his thoughts crouched in him and he reached out, switched off the computer. "Obvious! God, I'm slow."

He let himself down onto the floor in a semi-controlled fall, which was more violent than expected. He rolled onto his back to find his body. He wondered if he was still inside. Yes, inside the body and aware of things inside his mind.

In the caravan, he saw the familiar electric blue imprints, rose imprints! And the same silver sparkling ignitions of stars he had come to know over the past year, starting so far inside their souls that the significance they imparted in the tiny hot flashes of light felt as though it reached beyond the earth to designated constellations, specific pictograms in the heavens. He recognized the presence of the gods.

F—Fehu, sheep, cattle, money, food, power, new beginnings.

# 9. Indian Summer

"THIS MUST BE HALLOWEEN!" SAID JOHN, observing that Bellarose trailed a tail with dark furry rings interspersed with orange.

As she turned and looked him in the face, it was as though Egyptian mythology had tumbled into the present with all its human animals. Now, before him, was obviously a woman in the image of Bast, the cat-goddess, mother, dancer and lover. Instead of rings and jewelry, this one had stripes.

The two men began to caress her in wonder. The fur was not entirely fur, but seemed on closer inspection to be made of light. A fact which brought with it a renewed understanding of a light that had been filtered out and forgotten in the social human world. This was luxury. A sensory experience that developed while they recalled who they were.

Each caress aligned them with each other. At times, they discovered that they were all growing more catlike. The vehicle of the soul was simplified, while memories of similar past events returned.

The desire for a more human caress brought the hands back from being paws. All the while, they were in telepathic harmony, the caresses circulating the ideas, the memories.

Out of their sexual embrace, they had continued with John on the slipstream. He was, of course, ecstatic to see them wake up to the happening with him, to share it all. Bellarose's fur was balancing them out.

They discovered that, as she moved, the fur suggested hidden colors that were suffused throughout this astral light body and almost seemed to surface like an impressionist painting of far off scenes caressing her likewise with familiarity before riding away along waves of light, calling to their attention her aura and then farther and farther out into the distance, her vast aura.

They realized that they, also, were connected to the environment in this intimate and far-reaching way. Every move she made, every position, every pose was in the language of the art along the stream.

"You're a walking exhibition!" the photographer exclaimed, using a threshold of telepathy that gave vent to vocal chords and the first verbal conversation in out-of-the-body sound between the three.

"Post-impressionist," added Jesús with a smile, scratching his chin.

She began to purr.

They were astonished. She had sometimes looked as though she might be able to purr, but this was it.

"Is this the real you?" asked John. "I mean, when you're expressing yourself, totally relaxed, exactly the way you are, this is how you get, right? This is you being you, isn't it? It's amazing! It's really who you are! This is Bellarose, the cat! Hey, Jesús, look! It's Bellarose!"

John was materializing with impact. In the midst of his excitement, there was a white flash of light.

Jesús watched in awe as John crouched down by Bellarose's side and put his head against her womanly thigh. She tousled his hair.

Tickled and shocked, Jesús realized he was looking at a sphinx. "You're a sphinx!"

"So are you," came the lazy reply. The two looked at one another, mystified.

Bellarose reached out her hand to the Jesús sphinx's nose. This gesture aroused in him a sense of heaviness. He shrugged it off and stepped forward in his own image of Puck: as an irresponsible sprite, a trickster!—an excuse found the world over in many forms in many mythologies. The Raven, the Coyote, the Viking, Loki . . . and so with Puck, the god of the hearth. A trickster? But of course! Why not? What an act! To play the fool in the heart of responsibility, what freedom! Perfectly understandable, as far as Jesús was concerned, just the thing for a sojourn in the astral world, away from the cares of that Other Otherworld . . . whichever or whatever . . . anyway, it was irresistible to be so unreliable in the land of faith, where the gods dwell. To be one of them. After all, it wasn't like claiming to be the One God. Just Puck. Play a little hockey on the magic ice of the slipstream. Play Baal! Kick it around a little!

"Ah! That's better!" he exclaimed and extended his arms to her. She got down on all four paws again, though her physique remained almost human, the legs becoming surrealistically supple in catlike ways, and she circled round his Hobbity shape, mingled her lights with his.

She then rose up between his arms and kissed him again and again with her human cat-face, human lips and cat ears. It felt as though they traveled long distances with a troupe of actors in a short space of time.

John rested immobile, except for the continuous waves of effervescent colors that sailed through him from the tip of his nose to the tassel of his tail, as though enjoying quiet descriptions of distant fireworks by listening to a female messenger's bliss.

He felt like a compass aligned with a rose with its petals opening up. He realized that without the motion of the petals from the center of the flower, he would have no direction. That without his love of the petals of the rose, they would not open.

It occurred to him that a magnetic compass can sense and feel out the magnetic field of the planet, like birds in flight.

He felt the nearby brook drawn down into the Kennebec and down into the Atlantic by gravity itself drawn inwards and down into the planet by some deeper polarity within the electro-magnetic power of water transforming into vapor, into clouds, into rain. He saw ships lifted up by the soft magic of water where he could swim with such ease.

He recalled the way the soft magic of the slipstream lifted stone, and he felt at ease in its powerful gliding transitions, like clouds filled with potential, electrically charged within the gravitational field of the earth. He felt the sensual electrical energy and inhaled the rose.

Bellarose and Jesús turned to the sphinx. "It's a good thing he doesn't have one of those awful royal headdresses," she commented, as she played with the mane. "I think they were meant to imitate the mane of a lion. How phony these royals can be!"

"They have to be," said the sphinx. "You can't look down on everyone else and be at one with nature at the same time. As soon as you have a royal family, you automatically have an underclass. A cast system develops from there.

"Nature's democratic. The seeds of democracy are planted by the gods. We dream of heaven on earth, we have myths about a garden. We get confused. The political tension from Atlantis to the present can be summed up as the struggle for democracy, from the Sphinx at Giza to Robin Hood and the Magna Carta to the sudden embrace of democracy today . . . and the enemies of freedom are pressured like never before.

"It used to be their world. The change is so sudden, in fact, that it is driving them to extreme measures. We have been underestimating them. I am beginning to understand what is happening."

"First you have to be political with a sphinx," said Bellarose, and she threw her arms around the furry light, "then you have to act." She got up astride John's back, and the three of them walked out of an apple orchard.

"Looks like Uncle Sam's farm. We're still here," said Jesús.

"Thought you'd died an' gone t' heaven, didn't ya?" said John. "And here's the Manitou stone." He smiled and advanced to the smooth surface of the boulder that stood tall and wide. The smile radiated his aura upon the stone. The neck and shoulders rooted the expression in the muscularity of the body and its fabulous grip on the slipstream: receptive, resilient and secure.

The straight, bold nose of the human incarnation now swooped up into the face from a flat velvety ridge with nostrils comically enlarged to inhale the distances. It tickled him to be back at the beginning. It was all a maze, after all! And always different. Never just a circle. But a circle!

The enormous blue eyes of this cat laughed from the ever-breaking wave of the eyebrows that rose with abrupt soulfulness from the root of the nose to extend away gently downwards into the infinity of the mane that reached back into the slipstream, transmitting that light from the face onto the stone, acting out that image of a sphinx, allowing the god, Baal, to merge with John's soul and look through those eyes.

The teeth, Bellarose noticed, were white, human, but sharpish. And the jaw was naturally large enough to balance and blend the lion-sized head with the lion's body. A dimple twinkled between the angle of the jaw and the curved landmark of the cheekbone, a star on the waves of laughter lines.

As he looked into the standing stone, he looked out into the Hall of Symmetries. He could see the crescent-moon table and the backs of the seated hierarchy with the Grand Master in the middle. Just beyond, on a star-shaped platform, the sibyl was channeling the voice of the one whose traditional image—the empty skull and its crossed bones—flanked her inside monitors on the pentagonal dais. Unaware that Baal was with him, John listened to the words of the oracle of Baphomet.

Beyond the throne, he could see the mural of the Symmetry of Obedience. He admired the artwork. But the scene of such a multitude on its knees made him look away. Not without noticing that they were staged in five levels of kneeling people, some above others in time or in status. It was strange, incongruous, against the natural setting of the Tor. And the absurd little group having a "good time" beneath it all, in mock similarity to the select gathering of Ascended Grand Masters rubbing shoulders and being good fellows with the Buddhas, Krishnas and other chosen Christs at the top, where the ruined tower of St. Michael's Church would have stood—

He saw once more how impossible it would be to kneel down before Baal, before Puck. A self-contradiction with nature's gods, individual souls like any other soul with experience to share, to be shared in a loving manner. They would not encourage this!

From within the stone, he clearly heard another voice: "Kneeling does not teach love. Kneeling down teaches the opposite: selfishness, the false humility of the sacrifice program. It is a statement of credit and debt, the balance sheet alone. It tries to make a servant of the master and makes beggars of them all!"

While John wondered who had spoken, his attention was arrested by the sight of a man standing with one foot ostentatiously pressing forward in a shiny black shoe onto a red tile that bled along one arm of that cross in the white marble, away like an artery from the rose pattern surrounding the dais and its throne, away to the Symmetry of Terror.

The man stood, statuesque, halted there like a servant with his silver platter.

John noticed the remaining slices of meat, as though there had been an interruption. The Master was gridlocked on the red line, where Jack had said: "Wait!—"

Clearly something was wrong with the ritual flow of the occasion. The voice in the channel had become increasingly intense, losing its sophistication, but seemed to summon the energy to remember its lines, desperately, as though overcoming an adversary in a final struggle where everything depended on having the right words at the right time. As though time were limited. It was addressing the Master on the red tile. "I have singled you out, each one: you will not fail!"

It turned again to the crescent. "From the Arians to the Cathars to the Jews and fifty million dead in one generation and millions in starvation day by day... They have tasted the Sword of the Apocalypse. It arrives on waves of blood, waves that build and build . . . They grow like red flowers in the desert, impaled for oil—they are sucked dry by the giant acupressure that stretches the neighboring Sahara Desert like a dead skin over the drum of Africa's doom. The trees are sucked from the withering soil in sacrifice to the oozing pressures of oil." The voice paused and no one moved. The sibyl's hand went up, the voice rang out: "I will brook no interference!"

John saw the flesh begin to wobble alarmingly on the bone, where the upraised hand laid bare the arm under the loose and gaudy regalia. The voice proclaimed, "Jack Bridges is dead! It is a matter of course that no brother will interfere with the slipstream. It is nature's law.

"The destruction of the cycles of the ecosystem from pollution, moral decay, selfishness and greed will bend the rungs of the maze back to the dawn of time on this planet! Back and back, my children!

"The Judgment Day will dawn! The Day of the beginning of the earth, the Day after the living encroachment is wiped fresh from the face of the planet, the Day when living things will creep forth in abject humility once more before the Creator, creep close to the earth, begging forgiveness, begging for one more chance, one more time.

"I, Baphomet, will hold that time in my hand.

"Shortly, it will be accumulated there in the manner of the serpent. It will dally before it springs to renew the earth once more. I, Baphomet, will have squeezed the essence of the word until time itself stands still! For when everything is at an end and nothing moves and there is not a sound, not a pulse, nor a beat of the heart in the universe, then time is no more . . .

"I will squeeze it and squeeze it with the serpent power!"

A red ooze dripped from the elbows onto the silks. Both hands were gripping the air. "When time is no more, the maze becomes one and explodes in the colossal silence!"

The body sagged. A stench of putrefaction burst into the nostrils of the brothers. John noticed that a light had gone from their bodies, leaving them seated like a tawdry row of leftover guests at a costume ball. He saw that there was now a sphinx looking out of the monitors where the skull had been. The look of surprise looked back at him. He widened his eyes at himself. "That's me all right!"

Then he looked down at the table. One of the Masters, standing up, struggling, was pointing at the screens.

The sphinx was looking down from the screens at the disruption. The man wheeled and pointed into the mural behind him. John recognized the face of the Secretary General of the United Nations,

Jesús's father. He heard the man's words and saw him struggle towards him. "It's . . . in the Symmetry of Rule!"

The brothers were up and out of their ornate chairs. They looked up at the mural. They saw only the painted image of a sphinx. Then they looked down at the Grand Master's body, dead on the line of red tile. They realized that the slipstream had backed up on them. The realization continued as they went into shock.

The scene disappeared from John's eyes, and he was again looking at the smooth surface of the standing stone, wondering.

He thought of the people who had worked to polish that surface so smooth and soft. He reached out and placed a paw against it. He stretched out his claws and wondered at the whole business of being a cat and then considered briefly the point of view of a sphinx. "Why?" he wondered yet again.

"This is still the old farm," said Jesús. "But there are many differences."

"This is it, all right," said John.

"The stone?" said Bellarose, getting down off his back.

"I wonder what's on the other side," said Jesús.

"I'm almost afraid to look," said the sphinx. Cautious of his own reactions, he crept round the left side, while the other two crept round the right. They looked down nostalgically on John's earthen body.

"I suppose we're all dead, after all," said Jesús.

"You're always so sure," said the cat of Bast ironically, as she knelt down and gave the sleeping body a kiss. "I don't know about your body, but this one looks just fine to me. Just a little tired out after such an eventful morning."

"It's getting to be lunchtime by its watch," commented the sphinx.

Jesús leaned back against the stone and stared at an apple tree. "It's apple-time."

John looked down at the sugarbush. The leaves were turned into the flames that connect autumn to eternity in New England. They filtered the sunlight with such radiance that they climaxed as he looked from one group of trees to the next. It sugared him with sex. He felt the climate change.

"It's going to be hot!" said Bellarose.

"An Indian summer," said the sphinx, and he was gone.

They watched him reincarnate and awaken inside the human body against the root of the stone. It was as though he had died.

R—Raido, journey, quest, wheel.

# 10. Down Home

JOHN HAD GONE FOR THE TRACTOR, while Bellarose watched over the sleeping body and kept the bugs away. Jesús was still unaccounted for. The brook ran at a good pace; there were pleasant breezes, and the slipstream was now stronger on the farm, dispersing some of the martial arts of alien insects, like the mosquito and black fly.

She killed one and considered the importance of priorities in protecting the ecosystem. It was obvious that people had to figure out what this "nature" was and not just go around saving it at random, which amounted to a disguised attempt to control it, scavenging credits. "They'd end up with the anti-environmentalists, obsessed with controlling freedom with lots of flag waving while trying to manage nature as a means of destroying it. They destroy themselves in the end.

"Next thing you know some of 'em will get together to promote the protection and spread of certain favored childhood diseases.

"And how to understand the relentless attacks on the National Parks and forests? A matter of principle? Filled with that all-American hate—and proud of it?"

With these thoughts she lay down and tried to rest her head on the shoulder of the sleeping Jesús, cuddling up against his naked body, where she could reassure herself with the rhythm of his heart. After a while, it mingled with the vintage diesel engine as it came pumping up the field.

She got up and dressed, and she and John dressed Jesús. They lifted him onto the old wooden trailer and made him comfortable with a blanket. "What'll we say happened to him?" she asked casually, aware that the issue could take on almost any size.

"Drunk?" said John.

"Dead drunk?"

"Let's hope not."

She leaped into the worn curves of the steel driver's seat and wiggled appreciatively, "Hang on!"

John was aboard with Jesús, expecting the ups and downs of that terrain to jog his old friend's memory back into its earthen body. They traversed the hundred acres to the barn, and he was still asleep, or so it seemed.

Three fast children were around them, as soon as the ignition was off. Over half a dozen others wanted to climb up with Bellarose. "Easy, easy!" John was saying, "Look out for your knee on his face! Careful there, he's still alive!"

This attracted the others, except for the two who had made it all the way up onto their mother's knees on top the tractor. And a third, over from town for the day, half way up the great cat's leg, demanded that it was already her turn to be up on top with the maternal animal on the dragon machine. This insistence attracted another small cub to the other human cat leg. John was calling for help.

Samantha came down from the porch. She looked into the trailer: "Not him again."

"Disgusting, isn't it?" said John. "You'd think he could at least make it into his new family on his own two feet!"

"What's he got this time? An accident?"

"He'll be all right in a few hours. We'll just lift him into bed and let him sleep it off."

"Drunk? I always knew he was a lush." She lifted her eyes to the hills. Some of the kids looked up at her Native American expression for a moment. A beautiful instinctive knowledge of the landscape could make newcomers of them all, fresh with the gift of discovery, still to be received by more Christian invaders.

There was hope for an performance, a story. Sam had traveled a lot. She leaned over and sniffed. "Don't seem drunk to me—addicted to something, more likely. They used to lie like that—" She looked at the kids and raised her eyebrows with a warning, "You know, under the empire!"

They remembered the story.

She smiled reassuringly. "No, it's not drugs, either." She eyed them with a challenge. It was a guessing game.

"He's asleep!" said an eight-year-old boy, as though arriving upon a treasure.

"Everybody wake him!" joined in a little girl, over with her brothers from a neighboring farm.

As though it was everybody's idea at once, a chorus of "Wake up! Wake up!" washed over Jesús to the drumbeat of many small hands and the rock 'n' roll of an accumulating game of push and pull until the body was in danger of becoming a rag doll on a washboard in the burgeoning band.

Finally he woke up.

"So, what's the story, what took ya so long?" said John, laughing and relieved.

"You wanna know the story? Listen to this." He sat up in the trailer looked round for the audience and stretched with his hands behind his head, yawning. "Hi kids! Hi Sam . . ."

"Well, after you left . . . Bellarose and I had an encounter with my father."

John leaned back against the wooden fender of the trailer.

Jesús tried to launch straight into the tale. "So this animal here," he was poking at Bellarose, "was about to claw him to death, when I intervened."

She surveyed him closely.

"No, in reality, I simply felt that after the last encounter it was for me to make a statement. She'd taken enough flack already." He beamed back at her foolishly, detecting a sigh of boredom from the kids.

Assuming a distant look in the eye, he continued. "I was taken to an enormous circular domed temple in the clouds."

He paused for effect and felt the magic take hold. "Once inside, I was released in a large, square room with many doors. I was told by the beast that each doorway led to the Kingdom of Heaven, that no matter—"

"Stop!" said John. "Beast? What beast."

"I'll tell you later." He looked round at the kids.

If he wasn't going to tell them about the beast, it was probably an adult story, so they wanted to know.

"That no matter which door I chose, I would be brought before the One God, where I would be judged."

"The One God?" said Sam with a yawn.

"I had a choice: I could remain forever in the square room, or I could go before the One All-Seeing, All-Knowing, All-Powerful God in Heaven. Any door would lead to His throne; I had only to choose!"

He called upon his French accent ever so slightly. "Well, my family and friends, I can't say that I was honored! Without delay, I opened the nearest door. I stepped out and found myself in the desert.

"The beast with large, oblong, bulbous eyes was still by my side. It told me that I had been judged, that I was lucky. I had been granted extraordinary powers in order to satisfy myself concerning the extent and knowledge of the Lord of Creation. It was a great opportunity I was being given, it was the Holy Grail, and the beast handed me a goblet. It was very ornate and I felt obliged to accept."

He straightened himself and began to gesticulate. "As I held it, everything about me turned into radiant light. I was blinded except for the radiance."

He squinted up at the sun.

"I could not feel, hear, smell or taste anything; my senses were deadened. Yet I clung to the cup for dear life and drank the radiance down. I became a ball of fire in the cosmos.

"This is how it felt, I tell you, sitting here, but I still have no idea what was really happening. I can only tell you, you who are close to me, what I discovered on this quest.

"A vast question opened in my soul: it was a thirst for the unknown. I was desperate to quench it with the cosmic answer. You cannot know what that burning fire was doing as it ravaged my senses. Listen carefully when I tell you that I did everything I thought possible and I went everywhere I could to put out that fire that was consuming me, torturing me. When, finally, I came to what I thought were the limits of my powers, I fell exhausted again in the desert.

"Nearby, I perceived there was a box."

He paused to get his breath.

"I dragged myself to it and opened the lid. There was an eye looking back at me. It was without any expression whatsoever except for two awful words that it said to me: *'Hello there!'* "

Some of the audience giggled.

"It saluted me just like that: *'Hello there!'* "

The laughter dried up, except for a joker who called out, "Hello there!" After which everyone felt uncomfortable.

"So hurry up with your story," said Bellarose, "we haven't got all day." She was suddenly fatigued, her eyes watering as she tried to wipe them dry over and over.

"Go on," added Sam.

"It's important for you all to know why those two simple words became so terrible so quickly that I have come straight back to tell you the story of the One God. Here among you, I hope to heal myself."

Some of the kids looked at him skeptically; he seemed to be in working order, except he was being a little weird.

"I dropped the lid and backed away from the box. An anticipation of evil came over me, and I began to run in the desert.

"But I stumbled over another box. As I sat nearby, I thought I would try again; perhaps, given another chance, I would find the way out of this riddle.

"So the burning question was reignited, as I opened the box. And there, as before, was the eye. Again it said: *'Hello there!'*

"I ran with renewed power. I leaped and flew like a shooting star into the cosmos. My speed was so great that as I witnessed the planets go by and the earth disappear. I found myself now in the black desert of space.

"I felt that surely I must be at the end of the universe. In the dark I saw, by the burning flame of my questioning soul, a further box. I had to open it. There was the eye! Like a repetition in the desert, again, it said: *'Hello there!'*

"Three times it had greeted me, and then the truth began to dawn. It came with a shock, the first bitter taste of suspicion.

"It came in the form of a question: what if . . . what if, no matter how far I go, there will always be the eye? What will happen to my horizons, if always there is the eye and always it greets me with *'Hello there!'* Where will I be?

"Then the horrible suspicion dawned further: will I, too, be looking out of a box?

"Friends! Family! Do you understand?

"I had to test this truth, even if it brought the dawn of an eternal horror. I was burning to find out.

"I took the challenge, discipline by discipline. I began with the quest of the mathematicians who built the pyramids. Sure enough, no sooner had I begun to conjure the number line than it formed patterns before me; crystalline shapes of complex relationships between different types of pyramid developed themselves into mathematical worlds to discover, opening out like the data crystal. I entered therein, fearing the worst! I went as deeply as I could go. In the end, there was the box and the eye and again it simply said: *'Hello there!'*

"My friends, my family! Tell me: what if it knows! What if it knows all?

"I had to be sure, although, as this horror dawned, it was, with stultifying, suffocating mercy, snuffing out my questioning flame.

"I embarked on further quests. I attempted to explore the pristine, inviting new horizons of worlds perhaps newborn. But the same tragedy was always there. Two worlds were enough to destroy any hope that I might experience the genuine excitement of discovery.

"The hope that, in my soul, there could be any genuine creativity faded, as the walls of eyes gathered in a masonry of boxes and built walls to box me in. In here, how could I, alone, have soul enough to make a single discovery?

"I searched for a door. Until the masonry was complete, doors in the walls were yet to be found. I would rush through on my hopeless quest to find any creativity in my own poor self. Was I nothing but a machine? A mere habit of being, a program?

"I found canvas and paint. I attempted an original work of art. But in the center of the canvas there appeared a box. On the side of the box was my painting already complete! I turned my eyes away, but in my mind I heard the words: *'Hello there!'*

"Who was I?

"I found the pan pipes and played them with skill! You know how I love music. Music is love! But as I played, the sound was echoed in my ears: echoed *in advance* of my playing, as if to show me where every note could be found. I improvised and improvised with the very heart of my soul, but every note lay dead in a box; every single note said: *'Hello there!'*

"None was true, none was free, none spoke for itself in its own resonance, none was allowed to gush life's infinite fountains of love!

"I broke down. I despaired of being able to die.

"How could I hope to return to be with the ones I love? To be reborn!

"I would be nothing but a box within and among boxes: I would be like the One God looking out and saying: 'Hello there! I am here already! I already know! I am the All-in-All! I know everything, and you have nothing left to realize or discover! Just follow me like a sheep. I will be your guide in the desert! Don't think! Don't travel! Do not quest in nature! Look where it has got you! You have been torturing yourself! Take solace in me! I am your God, and there is none other before me. I am all. You are one in me, and I am love!'

"All lies and pieces of truth!

"Like a monk in my cell, I despaired of ever finding the farm, the garden! In my box, there was no infinite. Infinity could not exist without horizons of creative discovery! The truly Unknown! Free horizons!—"

"So God is a communist after all," said John.

"And a sarcastic little Nazi," added Sam. " 'Hello there! We are SS, and we would like to ask you a few questions!' "

Jesús strengthened his French. "I thought to myself, maybe if the eye would just talk to me, just be polite, at least. Just be civil . . ."

"That must have put an extra shiver up your spine!" said Bellarose.

"Of course, you're right. Anything it said would only change the arrangement of the boxes, so to speak, try to build an illusion that I wasn't in hell."

"So how did you get free?" demanded a little girl.

Jesús looked her in the eyes, "You kids saved me."

N—Nauthiz, need, primal fire, introspective challenge.

# 11. Culture Shock

"THAT'S WHAT I WAS GOING TO tell you!" shouted Lawrence. "No credibility! None!

"Why don't we go to the chief an' tell 'im what's in that box over there? Why? Cannot! Why? Because none of the likes of us 'as it, know wot I mean, mates?

"Your spymaster out there in the middle of the day would as likely believe the moon was shinning brightly over 'is 'ead! Take my meaning? They believe anything! They believe nothing!

"An' 'ere I am with a bleedin' window on infinity an' the world in the balance! Me? You? How 'bout we just sort o' team up an' go off t' market like a right foursome's been starin' into a video screen for a bit longer 'an's good fer 'em, see, an' then why don't we just tell the preacher-man where it's at, now, an' what 'e can do wit' 'is espionage network an' we'll see 'im at the reception! Know wot I mean? 'ello 'ello 'ello!" He looked at the other three and continued.

" 'Ere! meet ol' what's-'is-name! No cre'ibility! 'Ere it stands and does all right by it, too. All right for some, Jack. *Ahrtist.* All right for some! init!

"So 'ow'm I doin' mates! Am I outta 'ere, like before? Just walk out on me friends an' a good-day to ya, Jack! Julie! Tanya! Sorry I 'ad t' walk out on ya like that an' spill the beans! Come up sometime an' see the bullet 'oles in me canvases!"

He was pacing up and down on the patio.

"For goodness sake, Lawrence," said Julie, "calm down. There aren't any bullet holes in your canvases, and we haven't spilled the beans, yet. But, couldn't we arrange for a small demonstration, just to be sure? Who knows, maybe someone will buy it? Isn't there anybody we can trust? A little . . . with our lives, maybe?"

"Possibly a sex video of dancers round a maypole would save us?" said Jack.

"How 'bout a dancing bear?" suggested Tanya.

The artist joined them down on the steps that led into a small garden where yew, wisteria, magnolia, climbing roses and honeysuckle kept the lawn lush in its own private English climate. They looked up over the Chalice Hill and watched the light on Glastonbury Tor. Throughout the summer at this latitude, the shadows would take their time in lengthening while the sunlight in between would stretch itself dreamily and glow golden from within, lavishing care and attention on the landscape, later and hotter this year than ever, it seemed, now disappearing between the long black stripes like a mythological tigress slowly awakening, finally to slip away beneath the moon before you realize that night is here.

On the eve of the equinox, they had found each other once more, while the slipstream continued to open up, releasing tension.

They felt the warmth of the flagstones. "We all just ran away from it all, didn't we?" said Tanya. "Maybe that's what happens when there's no commitment, like you get in weddings, a promise, a vow?"

"An oath?" said Jack, restraining himself.

"The reason," said Lawrence, "why we couldn't keep it together is because we're wanderin' all over the place, can't stay on track. Now about this machine . . . we don't even know who knows we 'ave it! And the only one we know knows, we can't seem to tell 'im from the machine anyways!"

"You got it," said Jack, "The machine . . ." he faltered.

"The machine," joined in Tanya, "is a truth-seeking path-finder, OK? Even if the gods themselves lied to it, even if its inventor gave them all the credit in the world for having inspired its creation, and they all declared God Almighty the creator of all things and, like Michelangelo's mural of that little ol' Creator with one hand creatin' the moon and the other one creatin' the sun and God's own perfect little butt pointed in our direction, the very asshole of the universe and shit source of any data crystal the system might try to grow, and so therefore whatever that One God thinks or shits becomes gospel truth now, leadin' the system to answer questions with that truth, well?—still, don't ya think that the original path-finding software would overcome subsequent programming and discover the lies, discover that God is not who the powers declared him to be, that in fact God just happened in the Middle East, in the West, nothing but a myth, and we can't face it, that for two thousand years we've been worshipping and dying and enslaving for a mythology that we're just addicted to. I mean, shit happens! All right? Well? wouldn't that machine, like any good technology, stay true and eventually amend its records, given enough time?"

"They'd have to rip its guts out to stop it, gospel truth," said Jack.

"They'd lose all that credit for putting science to work in the service of religion, if they did that; I mean, they wouldn't be real bona fide usurpers, would they?" said Julie. "They might as well, if they did that, just come up with some weird God video and mix that into their orifice chronicles, don't laugh . . . claiming it's the word. Shit Tanya, how can we think straight around here, when you're givin' it to us so straight like that!

"Anyway, it's like what they'd accuse us of doin' . . . Like ya said, Lawrence, so who's got the credit, huh? Where'd it go?"

"Sounds to me like the Ol' Boy needs a good compostin'," quipped Lawrence. "Religion o' pollution, kissin' arse."

"Gives a whole new meaning to puttin' your ass on the line," said Jack, "or the altar, for that matter."

"So who's the butt of another joke, then?" asked Julie.

"Any more of that," said Jack, "and we'll have every tourist nudging the other in the ribs, sayin', ya heard the one about God?"

"I thought that was his face lookin' down at us from the Sistine Chapel ceiling." Julie looked at her guilty lover.

"That *was* his face," said Jack.

"No shit!"

"No, shitfaced: we get to witness the creation of the sun and moon, fore an' aft. If ya don't believe the one, maybe you'll believe the other? Courtesy of Raphael, Michelangelo, different works of art, one act. But it's a fake all the same. Never happened. Don't know why the artists bothered, frankly. It's all overdone, anyway. Someone must have felt they lacked credibility—"

"Or money?" offered Julie.

"Of course, ya don't wanna forget their sense o' humor. All them fleshy bums bouncing round in the sky—Lawrence?" enquired Jack. "I mean, no one believed it was God, did they? Did they? So who was it supposed to be, then? A typical god? A Serapis and company?"

"So the bearded face is full o' shit after all, said Julie. Well, that's no relief—"

"Actually, my dear," said Jack, changing his voice, "professionally speaking, that's one cybertype panoply B3, don't you know? A little bit flaky, I'm afraid. Had to renovate! God is back among us in living color, folks! Same Ol' Boy, just as he was created!"

"Give us a break," said Tanya.

"But, my dear, it's art, don't you know! Must be art! Simply has to be art! It's Michelangelo! Haven't you heard? Raphael? And who are you to say otherwise? I'll bet ya didn't even know . . . that Michelangelo . . . was Van Gogh . . . so! No culture credits, for you, my dear, unless you happen to be one of the ones . . . to know, you know . . . who's who . . . so who are you?"

She gave him a shove.

"No!" he replied, "the culture shock is out there. Not just in here. With a wavelength to match history. Which means: who gives a shit? That's the shock."

He felt like laughing but couldn't. "There are those who do care, but guess what? They care because they're filled with hate!

"Or, maybe it starts with a few bad jokes. Then people start to realize they've taken vows instead of logically following through with the truth? I mean who the hell's seen God? You're right, give us a break! Get off it! In an age of information technology? Sorry! Superstition."

"As a matter of fact, I would like to know," said Tanya, "who in this world has personally obtained one piece of evidence, persuasive evidence. I don't ask for proof. Just good evidence for the existence of that One God. An' I hate bein' evangelized!"

"There have been numerous instances," said Julie, "where people have felt or experienced something they must call God. But you know, you are absolutely right, they will never get the evidence they need to say: 'This is the One God for sure! This is not just any god whose countenance I have experienced! This is the One, the only one! And I would know if there were such another as this! Nothing can outshine this one god! I know that for sure!' " She looked at the others, wide-eyed with the discovery.

"Proof," said Tanya, "It's beautiful. That would be putting yourself above any god, including your own. Why Julie, that would be downright blasphemous!"

They sat together on the steps in silence, feeling the tension in the air shift as though trying to recover its lost ground, trying to push or pull them back apart.

"People have cut themselves off from each other," said Jack, "boxed themselves in with promises, promises to stay together and never to be with anyone else, promises to the lodge where no wives are allowed, promises not to blow the UFO cover-up. And even denials that they have made promises. So it's all come unstuck. Time goes on. Most people have seen the UFOs and the crop circles. Behind the promises there are silences.

"So one fine day, it has to happen, the Secretary General of the United Nations hoiks himself up from behind his Egyptian modern blocks in the Assembly, with the giant trapezoid dolmen to his back, and leans, convincingly enough, over the altar where he sits off to one side, of course, seeing's how he's been chosen by the guilty few, and all that ugly green nature-sucking marble, the gross squashed mural of a maze on the wall, the royal churchy purples and reds, and guess what?—"

"Bloody 'ell," said Lawrence. "Always knew you had no design sense—"

"He drops a wee clanger: that the world community finally acknowledges the existence of the so-called UFOs or extraterrestrials and that henceforth all the cover-up is at an end, and all those government files are now open to the media and the public, now that we have a means of communicating with our friends from other races in the universe, etc. etc., leaving out any of the still-secret details of that system—ending with a discrete hype for the upcoming production of the first truly international soap opera to help us cope with the change, the *Orpheus Chronicles*.

"It's all quietly exploding. OK, folks, they do exist. We dreamed it, we feared it, it's true, the U.N. says so."

They waited patiently while he caught his breath.

"And so what's new?" He paused and looked at them each one. "A crazy banana rush to secure monotheism as the U.N. umbrella, the central pillar of global society; keep it together, boys, while the West still has the credit!

"Didn't Western communism go global? I mean, didn't it fail or something? Don't worry, so Marx and Lenin didn't happen to be divine. Wait'll ya see the one we paste up this time—this One God. You better believe it, woman!

"So what else is new in a program? Priests have always known that to get your god on top was to take control of the people, not to mention their rulers whom they would cheerfully rip from their thrones for the sake of the god of Thebes, the god of Memphis, whatever.

"So now we've got an entire planet of everyone's gods at the U.N., and here we are at the General Assembly, still in denial, trying to pretend it doesn't add up to a pantheon, a good ole fashioned pagan reality.

"Historians know fairly well when which Jewish sect took power over the others by deciding that the god, Yahweh, should become everyone's God, caught them by surprise round 500 BC, about the time democracy was on the move again with Heraclitus and the pre-Socratic philosophers. Around the time Solon was leading the cause in Athens. Round the time independence from the Etruscans was won on behalf of the Senate and the people of Rome. Who wants to remember that Rome only became an empire six hundred years later? For that matter, who wants to remember that the Etruscan women had more freedom? So there ya have it, Rome fell! Who remembered what? Is this a big deal to suppress half the sexual equation? Those guys went down gripping their dicks for dear life! I mean, it wasn't enough, was it? A man who puts women out of mind loses his imagination—his mind! The art, the culture, dead, finished!"

"Can't even wank off," said Lawrence.

"Unless you're gay or got alternative polarities," said Julie with a smile.

"And everywhere they look," said Jack, still on a roll, "what do they see? Barbarians, fer Chrissake! It's not like they'd never heard of freedom before! They did have slaves.

"Roman historians still recorded Solon's trip to Egypt, 500 BC, in search of books on Atlantis. When powerful leaders were researching democracy. The people were thinking about freedom once more.

"Among the Jews it was all happening all over again: people were saying that the true meaning of the chosen is to choose leaders for themselves. It was the old struggle: the Jewish pagans along with their old Middle Eastern gods lose out to the one good god guys who got stirred up again under that one good god Pharaoh, Akhenaton, who figured he'd just sort of simplify the priesthood and start up New Age communities for the elite, ya know, walk among the people? So, how to look good and discredit democracy at the same time? I mean, does a program forget the oldest routines? No way!

"Extremely conservative hierarchies are always going to be hypersensitive to those little nagging hints of freedom, especially female freedom—nag, nag, nag?

"I mean, how the hell do you keep a woman like Nefertiti under control? Build her a New Age city filled with her art? Then get a 'separation' and keep the city? Not bad, eh?

"With King Tut caput after that, Egypt almost comes apart. The dippy little experiment in democracy fails; everyone is turned off. It looks like they're gonna have to share the guilt of murdering the pharaoh on behalf of the people—and he might have been a god, after all? End of the Eighteenth Dynasty! What a bloodline guy this was! Had to be a god!

"After the revolution, it's up to the nobles and commoners to clean up the royal mess, as usual. A military family takes control, of course. They identify with Set, god of chaos. Seti I in his short reign brings along his son, later called Ramesses the Great.

"Everyone's kowtowing to gods, right? So here's this guy with no bloodline, so to speak, and he sticks these statues of himself in the temples of the various gods, same size as the gods. Can you imagine the number that one did on the priesthood and the people?

"What a riot! Suddenly the gods are on a human scale. Not just human, but common human. And they think this guy had an ego? Sounds more like a sense o' humor to me: he leveled the gods.

"What used to be a lotta heavy duty ritual is now suddenly pageantry, theater!

"So the slipstream, where nature's real gods ride, opened up into the lives of the people. Get it? Art, music, dance! Architecture—cool, huh?

"Every subsequent king to compete with that act ended up leveling himself and bringing the nature spirits to town, whether he wanted it or not, popes included."

"Like, what's that Egyptian obelisk doing in Saint Peter's Square, I wonder," said Tanya.

"Yeah, guess what? It's still happening! And right here at our own United Nations. The nature gods are still comin' t' town, in spite of the hierarchies. Because rulers want to outdo Ramesses the Great. Incredible!

"He was a commoner, okay, okay, an aristocrat. But guess what? Bloodline people believe divinity resides in *royal* bloodlines, right?

They can't comprehend it any other way. So how can this king who is supposed to be divine also be the grandson of the man in the street? He can't, can he? What does that make the man in the street?

"So he lifted a moral burden of belittlement, and with theater!

"It would have been a whole different kettle o' fish if this upstart had been of royal blood and stuck statues of himself in the temples like that. That's the divine right program attacking us now. They don't care about gods as individuals; they believe in hierarchy and succession, gods at one end of the line!

"Their royal blood is descended from the gods' royal blood. That's all there is to it. We can hardly imagine the effect of Ramesses' actions on these guys.

"So the question that burns quietly through the history of religion is: what kind of gods was Ramesses really with?

"Obviously, the same gods who wanted to demonstrate that love never comes groveling on bended knee. You just can't approach that way in a loving fashion. These are the gods of democracy. The same ones who didn't go in for being worshipped and stuck up on pedestals. "Sculpture, yes! Idolization, hell no!—

"So, you're a priest, scion of some illustrious family or other, you want to go to your local temple and worship some humongous icon of a god crafted by the local artists and stonemasons? You want to affirm your position as gatekeeper? But lo and behold, what have we here, along side the rest? A gigantic statue of the grandson a prole? The common man, made good? OK I exaggerate, but you get where it's going—the slippery slope.

"They were keenly aware of it, you can be sure. But what could they do? He had the power, the credit. The demon gods were checkmated by their own programs in history.

"There were plenty of resignations accepted and priests without a temple—with vengeance burning.

"There's a man in power who works for the people. He restores the health of the land and opens up trade. He reorganizes the military and they defend themselves against forces that had been building up to take over an Egypt bereft of a proper divine dynasty.

"Through strength and patience he found lasting peace with traditional enemies. He methodically broke down the old programs. Not bad, eh?"

He didn't wait for any response. They were thinking it over, giving him another chance.

"Check out the statues and the Temple of Hathor he built to the memory of Nefertari at Abu Simbel, by Nubia. The largest monuments to a Pharaoh's wife in history, on the border with a land where women had been accorded more power even than in Egypt, Nubia, the neglected civilization of the dark-skinned race. The system tells us that Nefertari channeled the gods.

"So, old Ramesses got the whammy on the hierarchies of the temples, something Akhenaton and Tut had failed to do. They never got over it. It became an obsession throughout lifetimes, down to the present.

"Consider carefully the added pressures if he is reincarnated one day and becomes Alexander—the Great? It's personally intolerable to some people wound up in all this, whether they know it or not. And it's all personal, affecting us all, because these guys have had power—that translates to credit. Whoever said ya can't take it with you! And bring it back!

"The Temple tries to store it up, money in the bank. Now they're trying to run the system off it. But nature grows back, and the gods and goddesses keep on comin' t' town, every town village and city, in some degree, you just can't seal them out, they touch wherever nature is. And we barely know the extent and the way of it.

"For example, back to Egypt, democracy wasn't possible anymore, but some tribes gathered together, many of whom had been enslaved in the wars and were set free during and after the revolution, and they leave town and head out with the dream still alive. Among them, naturally enough, were the adherents of the One God experiment and no shortage of unemployed priests!

"So, therefore, round 500 B.C., suddenly Ramesses is controversial again. The One God good guys go and write a scenario called *Exodus* more than seven centuries after the actual fact. In that particular soap opera, Pharaoh is definitely not one of the good guys: a worshipper of Baal, no less!

"Hey, guess where they got the Cain and Able story? Set and Osiris is one version.

"Guess who'd gone and established Set? Did anyone say this was some ant-eating hippopotamus god of chaos? With ass's ears, t' boot? Would Ramesses bring back chaos? What a joke! Yes, he had a sense of humor, but—who said this was the god of chaos and evil? So, where went the credit?

"For centuries the stories had gone the other way: how Set, who had long been a sun and sky god to the people of the Nile delta, a god of light, suddenly drops down and murders a river god, would you believe, Osiris, who undergoes a slight image change when he gets hung out to dry, chopped up and martyred in a mummy costume, losing his genitalia in the process, which just goes to prove that the wife, Isis, really did immaculately and miraculously conceive and give birth to little Horus, the falcon, who will henceforth symbolize the divine King of Heaven who gets mixed up with the mummy and comes to earth to save us and guide us while, to tie up lose ends, the sun in the sky becomes Set in the desert! Ha! Not bad eh? Same old-time number they did on Lucifer, which means light: switch 'em off, make 'em dark—"

"Definitely on a roll," commented Lawrence.

"So, who turns back on the lights? Ramesses the Great! And who does Set turn out to be with? Astarte! Ah ha! And Puck and Titania join the dance! Off come the asses ears! Whose illusion, boys! Enamored of an ass, my ass! Who's the servant and who's the king, now? And the bottom falls out of Oberon! Whoa! Will they take him up and down?

"Set therefore just turns out to be Baal? Ramesses does turn out to be with Baal, after all? As though Solomon and Sheba weren't trouble enough! And some of us still have to be Christians and Jews?

"So OK, so Astarte's a temple dancer—some say she's Hathor the whore, so what if she's with anyone? But, wait! Where's the theater without the husband? Where's Baal? Good ole JB? But he's Just a Bear! Ho ho, who's this comin' out of the sea? Neptune? Just another god?—

"Where's the act without the soul? Where's the art without the direction, the love, the personality without the expression!

"They dance on and on, and it's out in the open. It's the way! It just keeps on going back and back and back in time, back to Atlantis.

"You can hear the cries echoing down the marble temple halls: When will kings just be kings and stop tryin' things on! Well, at some point, I think ya either care or ya don't, and if ya happen to be king, you're at that point. So you might look for ways to help out . . . or not.

"So there's a long tradition of blocking what's natural by declaring some damn god as number one. It's the whole damn struggle of Egypt down to Antony and Cleopatra—and I don't know why the hell I'm going on about it!"

He gave the others a familiar worried look, wondering if he was off track or was this going somewhere, the way they had realized so many things before, until the pressures stirred up finally overcame them, and they lost the direction in each others images, until now.

"Why does it still matter? It's ridiculous! But it keeps on mattering because the present social programs are based on nothing more than a lie and a cover up. We all live in the dark. The dark of an age terrified some Ramesses will turn back on the lights, and we'll all be caught here with our pants down.

"You can have a look at how bad it is by what's left of nature on this planet—I'm sorry—"

He panted while they waited for him to finish.

"Curiously enough, today the Jews have found their democracy, so scholars are beginning to question just how many gods they really have. People feel something's in the air, it's a consciousness 'cause we're naturally sensitive to our own history: we were there, of course. And of course it was hell.

"So they're worried about the Christians. It's the same old reason for the persecutions: if the Jews get outta line, God help the hierarchies! As a people they carry the seeds of freedom. Yes, the god Yahweh was more than once accepted with his consort, Asherah.

"Already we've seen the headlines in the academic journals: five-year study concludes that an international pantheon would be the most favorable planetary environment for the spread of democracy. It's here, and don't the boys know it! Shock, horror! Save the Lord! Monotheism for all! It's the only way, and now, praise the Lord again, it's all possible! Yes we do have the technology—just in time to receive his angels on earth, the little ol' extraterrestrials, would you believe?

"What about the United States?

"No problem. It's only democracy by default. They'll forget to vote!

"Sure, we've tried everything else for thousands of years, as though we didn't know 'bout freedom and equality, love and sex, friendship—hey, we failed, OK? We give up, we'll do it nature's way for a while, all right? all right! Wave those stars and stripes, boys and girls!

"Heavy guilt trip? Anybody say I told you so? No problem,

because, yes, boys, we do have the technology. We'll be vindicated. We shall overcome. Amen.

"A quiet catastrophe.

"It's so hard for so many people just to utter the word, *democracy*. It's got all these weights and measures on it. But have the boys been able to control it yet? Cliché it? Shout it all over the place, shove it in your face? Too risky."

"Too many new ones starting up all the time," said Tanya. "All these newborns just drivin' 'em crazy."

"Enter Glass Farm! Established to precipitate the culture shock by uncovering and managing the advent of the extraterrestrials, while saving the day by presenting a technology that would confirm the existence of the One God with the ET's as his little angels, thereby fusing myth and machine for a New Age. Every day just turn on the news and hear those hallelujahs on the horns o' heaven!

"All based on the cynical belief that the people are so addicted to their vows, their illusions and denials that they'll kill to be told a lie, to get back to the old ways. Equality? With the wife? Ya mean she can fool around too? And with money? Forget it!

"Basic program: dominant male and self-sacrificing wife. What a team! Both sexes can play. The man martyrs himself at work and comes home to beat up on the wife and kids because he refuses to be accountable for his mistakes. All right!"

"Too right," said Lawrence in a half whisper, "and what 'appens when 'e learns that 'is program of action is based on a role model who 'as never even been martyred in the first place? 'E ends up lookin' like a right winging little fakah. And his wife might even leave 'im, then! All them martyrs is got an angle. They get no sympathy from me.

"They'd better keep a lid on, eh, 'bout the sacrifice an' all that: he's just a man—what's gettin' out in the Dead Sea Scrolls an' that—what might just slip out of that computer box of yours. Them skeletons is bound t' make a difference.

"I mean, it's his thing gum bob, init? That typical cybercult thing you was referring to back when you was drivin' us round the twist. It's in 'is and 'ers: a deep an' dirty lit'le secret, never to be admitted, not on their lit'le long lives. Once it's out in the open, the juice is gone, gone for the both of 'um—married couples cut loose in cyberspace! Look out sharp, kids!

"If the four of us should 'ave learned anything out of our little contretemps, it's that it's bloody useless trying to 'ide the truth and 'ope to be in love at the same time for the simple reason that when you're interested in what's true, you're makin' the discovery that you 'appen to be in love, right Jack?"

The other breathed a sigh of relief and put his face in his hands.

"So, 'ow, I should like to know, is a good Christian couple going to live in peace when they is both unconsciously 'arboring the great expectation that one day, just like that, they'll be reborn! And the great secret icon of their religion will deliver them into a family what's got the lot! But mum's the word, don't say anything 'bout it! Don't ask! Say it ain't true! I never said a thing—don't know what you mean! Why you lookin' at me like that? That's not wot I meant— You know what I mean! Bloody 'ell, women! I ask you! Whatever you say it comes out all wrong— Men are all the same— And so, down the pub. 'Ere's to the Day o' Reckonin'! An' we'll 'ave at the bastards, too right! Cheers, mate!

"No one has to tell them why they behave the way they do, and no one can, either. An' why's that? They don't want to know, of course! Knowin' blows their chances! It don't look right, do it, now? Not the right Christian image! And they don't need no sermons for that.

"Not if one day 'is young lordship or 'er ladyship takes possession o' the parish and the servants and all the rights of superiority over the lower classes as though them rights was natural born rights, divine rights. They digs in an' watches them soaps an' waits, reads them tabloids an' gits ready—for the Day!

" 'Cause nothin' in this world can make their blood race like that kind of a promise. What a day it's goin' t' be! Such a beauty to be granted a righteous superiority over another human being: takes all the self doubt away an' the stress in all them lit'le niggling social pressures buildin' up, the decisions and responsibilities, gives them such a fine even attitude o' self-confidence, now, that you got to witness it, me friends, believe me, to believe it, and no one's 'as quite perfected it like some of our English, where they move day to day like they's on some angelic narcotic, the embodiment of the sacred promise that the lit'le bastard what's shoveling the shit in 'is lordship's stables can very well prepare 'imself for and put on 'is ridiculous secret little airs all 'is bleedin' pathetic life in preparation for the day when 'e too will win the pools, an' I don't mean your common ordinary bet at the dogs! We're talkin' 'eaven on earth. That's where 'e wants it: cash on the barrel 'ead, mate! Not on the never-never; that's no 'eaven to 'im.

"An' if 'e 'as to die before 'e gets it? 'E's like t' kill for it, or let be killed, no mistake! Look at you Yanks with near 40,000 shot dead every year, an' no proper 'ealth care, t' boot! Leave the nation's 'ealth up to the financial services industry! I ask you, desperate, init? They turns and turn away, turn away! Got'a 'ave the underclass or all 'ope is lost. Even your present status in the village, lost! Your security! Lost! Nothin' above. Lord help us! Nothin' below, God damnit! Kick the dog, kick the kids, beat on the wife— Are the boys going to get respec' one day, behavior! civilization? or wot?

"So 'ere we 'ave the deepest buried secret of 'is miserable lit'le Christian soul: 'e thinks 'e'll be back! An' 'e acts like it. It's 'is addiction! The little blighter can't 'elp it 'cause it's true. 'E will be back, too right, Jack, an' 'ave another go! 'E's got the gamblin' fever, now 'asn't 'e! 'Course the lit'le fuckah thinks 'e's off t' hit the big jackpot this time round, seein's 'ow 'e's been practicin' so 'ard at it all 'is life! 'E's weakened 'imself enough t' be eligible. 'Cause 'is other dark lit'le icon is that it really isn't an equal chance all round: the table's rigged, now init? He wants t' sit where Old King Arthur sat! Ah! 'E knows a thing or two, 'e does. Been round 'nough fer that, 'e 'as. Just a mattah o' ingratiating 'imself with 'is lord an' mastah! Git in good wit the 'igher ups! That's the way. Keep shoveling that shit, lad! There's a good Christian now what's seen inside the club.

"So ye ol' trouble an' strife won't leave 'er 'usband even for the sake o' the kids. So they all try an' escape within four walls, livin' in terror, trying to control the others with morali'y and ye ol' fashioned payback! In the end, 'e's got 'em 'ostage, unless she's got a job or another man."

Three of them quietly wondered how they came so close to losing this man.

"We're down to the wire," he continued. "All these people over 'ere focused on freedom; the others swearin' they'll never let 'em 'ave it. The rest turnin' round an' round in circles in the middle, 'cause they just keep turnin' away, turnin' away—"

"All we gotta do," said Julie, "is find a way to get the system to turn the Temple over to the police. I mean, they're cannibals; they murder people and eat them, right? Well? So . . . who's worried about credibility?

"The system itself is a machine . . . Didn't we just say it won't let them get away with it, right Tanya? Lawrence? A machine?"

"It's got that virus," said Jack.

"Jesús? You mean, like the computer's connected to him?" She laughed, "And he's runnin' to central Maine?

"Hey, if the program gets lost up there and asks for directions, they might just tell him, 'Ah, sorry, can't get there form here." An' he can always try to philosophize locally, of course. As Maine goes, so goes the nation, or havencha heard?

"At least the system doesn't think the One God built it. Or does it place old Jesús above God? With God? I guess it checks up on what he thinks about it . . .

"Let's say he makes up his mind that in spite of the fact that his science tells him that God is nothing more than a fig leaf, still there is some mysterious higher priority, like the good of the common folk, that demands that God exist in specific ways, with rules for human behavior and so forth and so on—can the system be made to fool all of us all of the time? Did we ever settle that one, once and for all, any of us?"

"They've got a technology," said Jack, "and there's the internet. They're losing the One God; they're tryin' to use the system to rebuild him or re-enhance his image for the New World Order, so the whole world will just find it easier to say 'God' and not have to communicate and really use the information infrastructure to think about and enhance their regional way of life, but instead just drop their stuff and go global, in a box—ya know?

"The ETs have the 'universal-one-mind-for-all' type mentality, so they don't care enough to go in for detail much, unless it's just for their image; so the question of the extreme long-term abilities of the system to figure it all out is really, to them, just a detail.

"These guys are all about havin' it now. They're rapers and despoilers. They live off the direction and energy of those who have the real creativity to attend to careful and significant details, the real craftsmen. That energy is creditworthy. So they block and take, block and usurp: it's all like a game with them, no soul, they really don't care, love is just credit.

"They'll just keep on playin' the system, harvesting from the people so much credit in return for the illusions generated by the system itself, programs to feed the popular addictions, until they have enough ongoing power to put off the day of reckoning forever. Or until it's hardly mentioned, just a detail. The powerful truth heavily blocked out by hierarchies.

"But the gods keep comin' t' town, and bloodlines die out. So they want to push back the time it takes for the system to unravel the blockages and illusions in the cybernet, push it, twist it, making so many delays and changes in the process that they eventually change the very nature of time itself. That's the power of the slipstream, and they'll kill the entire planet to usurp it, easy. Look at Mars.

"The Day of Accounting, which would normally be every day of the week, becomes the Judgment Day that never arrives.

"They won't get caught editing the system so it just looks like some artificial God video and everyone sees through their game; they've got enough cunning for that. But they'll go for the jugular if they get the chance.

"They intend to usurp time itself. Absolute power. All physical changes would be theirs to control. It's beyond belief. And still the system would continue to grow its data crystals, the Grail software would seek out the truth, but everything would be distorted.

"Again, forget about the details, think big! It's the big real-time, folks! The Temple would reshape reality, usurp the slipstream wholesale.

"People would go off on crazy quests and insane crusades, half-fought wars, massacres, genocide, brute force, but few outright victories, seeing as they are not really fighting for anything; it's all meaningless anyway, because it all depends on what they think nature wants. So they leave enemy elites in power or rearrange things in the family so it all starts up again.

"Phony judgment days would come and go.

"All would be propelled by outlandish rituals, where the moral masquerade replaces the truth, sacrificing it to feed the emptiness, override the disillusionment, the repetitiveness. A grotesque history would proceed. Sound familiar?"

"So, where's the power coming from?" asked Julie.

"People," replied Lawrence. "Suckers like us who paint murals on their temple walls and ceilings."

"It's the process that counts," said Jack.

"I recognized your handiwork in the Hall of Symmetries. The realization—"

"The shock," said Lawrence.

"Brought us together again," Jack affirmed, a hand on the other's shoulders.

"The temple dance?" suggested Tanya with a sexy mysterious smile, looking from one to the other.

Lawrence tried to return the pleasure.

"They expect you to give up," said Jack, "lose your sense of direction, like someone who takes out a loan and can't repay it. Their history is banking, after all. I know these people, believe me! Don't feed the program or it'll destroy you. You'll end up like Van Gogh.

"But if you do use your credit to open up the slipstream and keep on as an artist and quickly move to pay back your debts, keeping on with the gift, it backs up on them. Then, of course, you are perceived as a threat. The closer you get to the truth, the more they need to build a relationship with you, to control you. Things get complicated pretty quickly; like who are your friends and enemies? Especially with people getting sucked in by their weaknesses in the cybercult, looking innocent, just angling along and suddenly they're in the thick of it.

"With the four of us falling in love and with this piece of technology looming as a bigger and bigger secret that was finally going to blow open . . . well, they decided you'd better work for them. Put art in the service of the Temple. With me, it was science in the service of religion. Same thing, they befriend you.

"It's a dangerous game on all sides. It's back to Michelangelo and the pope, when the secrets of ancient freedom were getting free again, and the Church had become so laughable, being just a mask of masonry, half a Church, the other half grotesquely hanging out, it needed art, culture! He painted the pope's cybertype on the Sistine Chapel ceiling.

"Hey, even popes need to be 'Ramesses the Great' sometimes! So whose face is this? Up on a ceiling this time! Just another god?

"People began to say that Michelangelo was divine, a channel of God, more powerful than the Church, that he had saved the Church, he was a savior! The Holy Father was even forced to apologize to him on one occasion. The mouth of the painted God apologizing to the artist!

"So, whose illusion was it?

"Michelangelo di Lodovico Buonarroti Simoni," Jack rolled the syllables round with eye rolls over the Buonarroti. "Saves the ass of an institution that has the blood of genocide on its hands. A horrific irony to the finger of God reaching out to touch the man with a spark, and human flesh burns in the market squares. The artist knew it, callous bastard! The pope burned one of Buonarroti's favorite friars—the puritanical fanatic, Savonarola—right under his nose, looking to see how far he could push it. Lifetimes of guilt and over-aggression. Read those sunflowers! What do ya see? Art? Yes. Nature? Who can deny it?

"Ever wondered why there's reincarnation, by the way? Unfinished business—no joke. We run with Jesus until we get it, stupid! Then we run back to tell the others, shit!"

"Jesus?" asked Tanya, "or did you mean Jesús?"

"Are those Southern friars?" Julie deadpanned, adding, "It's getting somewhat dark. I'm still back with the Buonarroti. Maybe we should go inside."

"Either that or we get back in the car," said Jack.

"And go where?" said Tanya.

"Let's get back inside," said Julie. "It's beginning to look like the only way out. Welcome home, lovers!"

W—Wunjo, joy, peace, with Woden, Freya.

# 12. Love's Logic

"I DON'T WANT TO DISAPPOINT ANYONE HERE," said Tanya, playing with the ties on the front of her bikini top, "but I don't think there's going to be any knock at the door . . ."

"Continue," said Jack.

Julie responded by kicking off her sandals and, seated on the floor, stretched back over the lower of the two rolled-up futons that made up the living-room couch.

"You see," said Tanya, "already they've got us just where they want us, they think."

"Where's that, then!" said Lawrence.

"At the back door," she opened the front and arched her back, brushed her nipples lightly with her hands to make them stand out.

"Sneaking secretively around the back door of Slipstream Systems," said Jack.

"Round the back, Romeo!"

"So, we're just feeding the program," said Julie, sitting up straight. "A necessary part of the masterpiece!"

"Well I, for one, am a bit of an artist, when it comes to matters of this kind and not without some little experience, but never enough, mind you, which naturally brings me to a point, Tanya. You make a man want t' get down an' pray!" Lawrence moved in her direction on all fours, while she slipped from the couch to meet him.

Julie leaped up, "Well, we may as well enjoy it! I'm having a shower. Anyone join me?"

"They did try to kill me," said Jack.

"But they failed," said Tanya, pausing in her kisses.

"So don't fail us now, mate!" said Lawrence, looking up at him.

In a quick recollection of how things had gone down with the four last time round, Jack, nothing loth, opted for the humor over any offence in the tease. He cautiously went with the flow. "I guess they're into plan B, C or D. Bully 'em, kill 'em if you have to—failing that, have them for dinner. All style, frame of mind, practically no strategy. Can't be killed? OK, eat 'em alive! No knock at the door? Get ready for a formal invitation."

Tanya got up and followed Julie to the shower, "Follow Titania," she called back.

☙ ❧

The fulsome blast of hot water was bouncing off Tanya's back, off Lawrence's chest, and whenever the artist moved just so, it continued beyond to Julie's breasts, stomach and thighs.

Jack awaited his turn outside the ample bathtub in the steam-filled room, entertaining them with loud intermittent exclamations like, "Hurry up!"

Then, looking round the useless shower curtain that was directing more water onto the floor than into the tub, he could see plainly that Lawrence was in paradise. "Take your time!"

Lawrence grinned back through the soap, while the four female hands of the thousand-and-one fingertips, palms, fingers and grips brought him momentarily to speculate on the origin of the many-armed Indian divinities.

Although he responded in kind, he was vastly outmaneuvered and finally ejected towards the hot tub, while Jack was brought in in mid-exclamation. "At last, a real shower! I thought I'd have to go back to the States to find one. Maybe some people would just take this for granted, but for me, this is it, now I'm alive, I'm convinced!"

"Turn around," said Tanya.

While Julie rubbed the shampoo into his dark red hair and continued it down the back, between the buttocks and along the legs, back up again and then down with more suds from the top, Tanya washed the foam away and undulated the underside of his increasingly tight connection between worlds, flooding his imagination with each succulent hint of her fingertips and then finally her lips.

But after a preview and a taste, she kissed him goodbye, and he was sent to the hot tub as well, where Lawrence was already immersed in tasting the dreams that had rolled off Tanya's clitoris.

His eyes were closed when he began to feel her kiss him on the lips, softly, just making contact, sensing the luscious presence with much more than the edges of his mouth. Their emotions mingled, they understood one another and were at peace.

He moved his hand along her thigh, feeling the water and her smoothness over the hips; he felt a wave of sex break in his soul and follow the curve curling into her waistline to send his hand along the subtle ripples of her ribs to the side of her breast and the free back where he pressed gently while the wave awoke again and cooled him with a fine spray of slipstream energy, enlivening him in return to her touch. They shared the power of the slipstream connections made available by love.

The other two watched the kiss with total attention, each inflection of the translucent feel of the event unblocked their own slipstreams, relaxing them further, while their hands underwater joined in a firm gentle clasp of knowledge that sent bright electrical discharges of heat shimmering through their bodies, resounding quietly between them the simultaneous disclosure that the natural sudden polarity of their hands had made: the timing was so exact and the realization so unexpected in surfacing so soon that its familiarity came to them all new and magical and made them breathe deeply together in telepathic harmony.

Lawrence looked up at them.

"I've heard the word *love* before," said Jack.

"We're fucked for life," said Lawrence.

Tanya started to splash him, saying, "Here's another stage of our wedding ceremony!"

"But, hey! Shouldn't we have a ritual of some kind?" said Julie.

They all looked at her.

"Maybe it's just my upbringing intruding, but should someone actually ask someone, just to say it?" She leaned back with her arms behind her head and smiled at the alarmed look in their eyes.

"There she goes again, windin' us up!" said Lawrence with relief.

"Well 'ow else is a girl t' git one o' them kisses from ya, I'd like t' know! 'Ave t' threaten 'im now don't I?"

"She's speakin' your language," said Tanya.

"Say the word! But leave off with the rituals, please! An' as for your upbringing an' threatenin' behavior, allow me to translate my profound relief an' even me gratitude for the sense of 'umor you has shown, so that I might come a lit'le closer now and reach forth . . . first to come along the leg and 'oik meself up 'ere along the thigh . . . there that's bettah. Now if I might suggest . . . there, even bettah and oooo yes, now that's the way! Wot did she say 'er name was? That's the word I wus lookin' for! Julie, yes, Julie! Ah! Nothin' like it, is there, now!" He kissed her up and down.

"There's your natural-born ritual, Jack," said Tanya.

"Lawrence is so organized," he replied. "He's a mathematician."

She looked at the scientist and teased him with a sigh.

"No, it's true, look: sit up on the edge, and I'll show you what I mean. Here, science in the making."

"Love making?"

She sat up out of the water onto the edge of the cedar deck, and he looked into the hips and the mound of Venus. "Oh yes! All right! Now!"

She leaned back on her hands and opened her thighs while he moved to kneel in front of her. He began to run his hands over her form, about an inch above the skin.

Lawrence and Julie paused to watch.

Jack looked over his shoulder at them and then back, saying, "The thing is that if you look only at her shape evenly, just as a surface flowing this way and that, like an even field of energy, then you'd conclude that if I touch the skin here . . ." and he pressed his finger lightly on her forehead, "or here," he touched the end of her nose, "it should have the same effect as when I touch her here, for example," and he ran his finger along the top of her pubic hair.

"If I move down the smooth uniform skin of the tummy, logically, on the surface of it, you wouldn't predict the little surges, the building intensities of meaning and sensation as I reach here—" and he landed his palm down between the hips over the top of curly mound, emphasizing it. "But entire societies can be defined by the degrees of latitude given credit in this area of the female human form. Even though it's the same surface of skin as here, for example." He lifted a long sexy leg out of the water.

"It's logic like that what gets them all riled up," said Lawrence. "If 'er skin is equal to ours, not to mention the difference in color, then she can be as free as a man, in a woman's way—and that's hot. Equal means hot! Hot sex. Wit Haches!

"It has to be accepted, then, that she can turn on a man and 'e's powerless. There you 'ave it, mates or lovers or whatever you likes! Powerless in a male-dominated society, I ask you; can't 'ave that now can we! Not even a wee bit, not 'alf powerless; might set ye ol' egg over the edge! All the king's 'orses an' all the king's men?"

"All right, Lawrence! All right," said Julie.

He looked at her. "Mmmm, Julie, Julie, Julie! Ow, so good to me!" He started to kiss her again.

Tanya pulled Jack inwards. "You're onto something, aren't you, just like when we'd come all unstuck? But I gotta give it to ya, you've stuck with it, havencha?"

"And a fine fix I've got us into this time round!"

"But I believe you now; the system runs on sex."

"It's a tide. I touch you here, once . . . I return another time and touch you there again, and it's maybe not the same. The tide of your sex moves on the stream, beyond the body. You can move it around simply by posing or dancing. But a position held can be powerful, especially photographed. It can set up one hell of a wave—if the polarity is right. It can catch another wave, a carrier wave. The gods."

"And everyone's tryin' to control the gods: 'Get it just right, honey! It's a martial art, ya know!' Almost everyone?"

He kissed her along the fringe of pubic hair.

She took hold of his penis. "Why don't you come sit up here, and let me play in the water?"

"Do I have a choice?"

They traded places. She licked his erection and put her mouth over it a few times pensively. "Remember," she said, "what finally did it for me? That was the last straw!"

"First Julie, now you?"

"Relax!"

The other two were alerted by that change of atmosphere and looked over at the couple again.

"It was that infinity thing you did on my body with the indelible magic marker?"

"I told you I was sorry."

"Relax!"

Julie was at Jack's leg. Lawrence was softly touching Tanya's back underwater, at a loss for words.

"Right," she continued, "I told you I'd get my own back, remember? So let's pretend this is the standing stone, here." She separated his legs and gave the erection one more lick and held it between her breasts.

They heard Lawrence heave a sigh of relief.

" 'Ad me goin' there for a moment, Tanya!"

"Now we draw a little ole ley line here." Her finger traveled slowly round the base of his penis, tickling his balls, before ascending to his forehead, followed by the surprise of her breasts arising as she moved to kiss him on the mouth.

"Now the truth is that for this line to be truly infinite, it kinda diagrammatically goes all over the place . . . sorta like this! No other way to express it, really." She launched into patterns, licking him and tickling him all over until he tried unsuccessfully to restrain her from finding the right places that were making him go silly.

"Didn't know you was ticklish." said Lawrence.

"You see? Infinity," she continued. "Well now, listen up, lovers, we have to find the absolutely neutral point, equidistant between both ends, in order to bisect this line! From infinity to infinity? Infinity to infinity?"

"Stop!" said Jack. "Can't be done. We tried and it was a disaster! A disaster! remember? Wasn't funny! You had—a terrible time, remember? Stop her—someone! This could mean . . . our relationship . . . relationships!"

"Can't find it here!" she went on, "We can try here, here and here, bisect it here?"

He slipped into the water and she pounced on the wave. "But really, the only way to honestly do it is to make it back into a short or, let's say, a finite—line! So! There and there!

"What does this mean? As long as there's infinity, no neutrality! Unless we pretend to stop the infinity, there and there . . . at both ends!" She wiggled the somewhat flaccid penis. "You see, even if it's in neutral, it's always tending into gear!" She moved it into first, and held it to him in her palm. "Gotcha Jack, at last! Now, can we kiss the second law of thermodynamics goodbye?"

"Easy!" he panted.

She moved to give him a blow job.

"But wait!" He stopped her. "I think I've got it! A way out!"

She slumped back into Lawrence's arms.

"I guess the wedding ceremony is over," said Julie. "It's back to the real world."

"Not so fast," said Tanya. "Jack's got an idea—"

"By the way," said Julie, "before we get any further into the software, I've decided I want to hear a commitment, after all." She paused briefly for effect and decided not to press her luck. "If anyone's been out foolin' round since we were a family, I want to know about it. No STDs, please?"

They all shook their heads with weird remorse.

"Hey, that's it!" she said. "That's the trap!"

"You mean we almost got suckered?" said Lawrence.

They looked at him.

"Almost?" said Julie. "Want to tell us about it?"

"Nah, forget it, that's not wot I meant! I mean—"

"You know what you meant—"

"Wot, then? Orlright, so I'm a wee bit defensive; it's the murals, get it? It's the art, not the artful . . ."

"Sounds a bit dodgy to me," said Tanya.

"Seriously," said Julie, "I think we'd better make it clear where we're goin' with this thing. I mean I was onto something, right? And you all thought I was just havin' ya on, didn't ya? Well, what I really meant to say was that if we try an' go foolin' round behind each other's backs, then we're weakened, because we'll just be food for the program, just a part of the program, DOG food! That's what we all mean, right? There, I finally said it."

"What you were meaning to say all along? We won't hold it against ya," said Tanya, "because it's true, right?"

"I'll swear to that!" said Jack.

"It's self-evident," said Lawrence. "Swear to it or not, it don't change any of it. It's the way it is."

They scrutinized him.

"Well, I'll not be able to change it! That's for certain."

"Well, that's settled," said Tanya.

They relaxed into a circle within the wooden frame.

"We figured it out," said Jack.

"Took us long enough," said Tanya.

"I don't get it," said Julie.

"Let them talk," said Lawrence, "whiles you an' I— By the time we're finished 'aving sex, they'll 'ave figured it all out all over again. And another thing, whenever we're all in on it—"

"On what?" said Tanya.

"The back door thing, you know! What we was talkin' about—"

"You mean what's not worth swearin' to," said Jack.

"No, listen, it's serious, because the point is that if we all know, then we are all better off and a lot stronger because some of us sees things the others may not see, know wot I mean!

"For example, it might be the case that one of us gets himself or herself into a situation, just off hand easy, ya know, where there's another third party involved, if you follow me, like an 'usband who's wife is playin' games an' we don't know it exactly 'cept one of us sees it and can alert the other one who's just flirtin' and it shouldn't mean nothin', not nothin' t' us, except it does to 'imself or 'erself, what's got the addiction an' the thing gum bob, see, an' fails somewhat in 'is or 'er understandin' o' the situation, like wot 'appened t' us, remembah?

"So we kin enlighten ourselves and throw some light on the mattah. Know wot I mean, I mean, do you know wot I mean! You get sucked in just as easy now the one way or t'other, whether it's one of us you's foolin' or someone else's partner, get it? A dog's dinner either way you look at it. Unless you're addicted to that particular feast, it'll run you down flat pancaked, no mistake!"

"Just now, it's not the most seductive thing I've heard you say," said Julie, "but I take your meaning."

"I don't know what to say," said Jack.

"Well, we'll just have to explore," Tanya replied moving closer to him once more. "Love finds a way . . . through all the programs . . . You were saying?"

"Tanya, the cybercult is like a weather system. It pressures our minds and bodies. It pressures us . . . who we are. I've been a damn fool. OK, what that means is . . . for one thing, I've been laboring under the program . . . cybertype A1 . . . here we go again . . . look, it separates men and women and makes the men into the backroom boys. It pressures that way, at least. It gets to be a habit. You can be born into it and not see it . . . Here we go, I'm explaining— Basically, you've had the answer all along. That's the realization. The monument you've been studying—it's the answer. It's obvious. We met because you were on the monument's trail. We fell in love, but I was already in love with Julie, so I blocked you. You opened me up—"

"And all hell broke loose!" said Lawrence.

"Programs, cyber-storms! We've just got to accept it. They're real."

"And the system runs on sex," said Julie. "That's love, ya know . . . when you get down to it, no viruses . . . just love's pure pleasure, the logical thing to do: just love each other.

"Therefore, when you switch on the system, we're a part of it, really—" She paused.

"As long as it's on the slipstream with us," said Lawrence. "Now wouldn't that be all the time? The switch is just a technicality, wouldn't you say? Just a question of distance, time and degree?

"Of course, where its inventor is concerned, 'e's right in close all the time, so—"

"Why?" said Julie.

"Well, 'e's invented it, right?"

"Why?"

"Something's coming together," said Tanya.

"The only thing keeping us from realizing what we came together to do, is that which blocks our love," said Jack.

"That which was blocking us from putting the stage monument onto the system. Love wants it there, just like I want sex! With you, Jack. Or maybe Lawrence? What do you think, Julie?"

"I'm considering the question. Why Jesús? Who is this guy? You'd think he was God, the way they are trying to get the system to think like him and override all kinds of realities.

"You would think," Julie continued, "that the system could pick up on the historical Jesus and figure out pretty quickly that this creator inventor character is not exactly a top authority on the Almighty.

"As a matter of fact, come to think of it, you just got two real-world possibilities:

"One, the historical Jesus was what the Church says he was; in which case, when it comes to priority, the system would be hard pressed not to look to that Jesus first—wherever he is on the slipstream—and little ol' Jesús just becomes a maintenance man on the larger scheme of things, in the cybercult! The system would have him figured in no time! All his past lives, his panoply, all there to see. But it can't! What does that tell us, lovers?"

"What's the second possibility?" asked Tanya.

"Jesus is just a man out there somewhere on the slipstream. What then? The two are either one and the same or they are not.

"If they are, if the man in Maine is the historical Jesus—accent or no accent on the *u*—then the system can't identify him because it's got its own creator mixed up with the one they call the Son of God, who is mixed up with God Himself in some sort of Trinity that they never could get straight because there's no sex in their creation myth, anyway, no goddesses for the One God to date. A confusion that lets in all the blockages. Their theater—they like it that way, right?

"Now! If they are not one and the same, then: when it comes to following the mind of its creator, the machine has to check up on another mind, which it quickly identifies as another human being. So both are identified! Our inventor cannot be confused either with that historical Jesus or with God—unless its inventor/creator thinks otherwise about that historical Jesus—oops!

"But so what if he does? What if our inventor says that God is Almighty? And the program locks in that the historical Jesus must be the Son of God Almighty? So what?

"The system has heavy-duty evidence out there that this guy just can't be the Son of God. Like he didn't create the system; maybe he's living back in the States, or now he's a communist, or something—he's in society; his historical biography is clear; the hows and wherefores of his involvement in the religion are clear, all mapped out in history, as though he stepped out of the Dead Sea Scrolls or archaeologists found all his traces that gave rise to the myth and politics, just like they fear will happen, like you were sayin', Lawrence, the reality!

"That's too much pressure for one man and his computer to override. With all that evidence, the inventor would just be wrong. The system would just say no, sorry, that guy's living in China now. If you think otherwise and you're with God, then God's just another defect. You need to ask for help."

"Not what the Temple are looking for!" said Lawrence. "Not known t' be favorable to education, not for us, don't want us t' think it over too much. An' if someone's got to open up schools, they'd rather it was them!—"

"Well, then it's easy," she continued. "The reason why it's our friend Jesús confusing the computer is because he's just Jesus, that's all, got to be. Let's be practical. Computers, artificial intelligence, can't figure everything out—especially introspection."

"Well then, all we do now," said Jack, "is accumulate this whole conversation into the data crystal—"

"No credibility!" shouted Lawrence, hands raised.

"I don't believe this!" said Jack.

Tanya looked at him. "The Shakespeare Monument, Jack, please? Do it for the Dark Lady?"

"Talk about the system running on sex," he replied. "And talk about the fact that we are already on the slipstream with it in some remote way; it just occurred to me that we can't get to the button to turn it on without having sex somewhere along the way. Do I talk too much?"

"You know," said Julie, putting her arms around him, "I think it should have been obvious that we had Jesus online the whole time. Why didn't we think of it long before?"

"It's the gods," said Lawrence flatly.

"Let's face it," she pursued, "we were programmed all our lives, even though we never seen the inside of a church, not to entertain the possibility. We had to be here together. The way I figure it, this is not exactly an empty social program, being a family like this. But when the love is lost, it just becomes one. So the slipstream is opening up. We realized something fairly obvious that the machine never could in time."

"It's a turn on," said Jack, as she fondled him.

"And it's the gods, believe me," Lawrence repeated. "Sometimes you can realize something, but it's too soon. It happens all the time when you're painting. You stop, if you're going to be honest about it. You go and get inspired to do something else, maybe just the shopping or a bit o' gardening. Maybe you can't get back to the paints for weeks! Then it 'appens. You've connected the painting up with the rest of the world, and the statement is made, not just on your lit'le canvass, but in a larger picture you can't see. That's what makes art such a big scene, when you'd think that on the surface of it, it would just be taken more casual like, ya know? But no' a bit of it, not if you're inspired, an' that means doin' all them other seemingly disconnected things, but livin' wit' your art. That's the true professional." He smiled, eyes twinkling, reflecting the water in motion. "Break out of our programs with the gods, with a minimum of difficulty, if you know what I mean! Otherwise I'd be up in Scotland by now, onto my next canvass—"

"I'm hot in here," interrupted Tanya with a splash, "soooo hot. Anyone want to go outside, on the grass, under the moon?" She caressed Lawrence's sides.

Quietly they all rose together and glided back out onto the patio, down the steps and onto the grass that received them softly, as though touching from a distance.

They lay down in a circle, and Julie started to lick and kiss Lawrence and Lawrence started to lick Tanya and Tanya continued to lick and kiss Jack, who began to lick Julie.

Then they reversed the circle and lavished love and unspoken juicy language on the ones who had been pleasuring them, so that

Lawrence was now licking Julie, Jack having left off to lick Tanya who had been about to bring him to a climax but left off to take hold of Lawrence with a hand to her lips encircling, merging the animal in his mind, her tongue sending juices along the hard and soft surges of body and imagination, her fingers playing along the up-and-down rhythm every now and then.

They reversed again, all at once, without a word, awake in the same dream.

The circle began to open up here and there as they climaxed, releasing on the slipstream all the words they had accumulated, chords of music, sharing the waves of pleasure with the nearby presence of the Tor, ringing true with its own history and direction in the maze, where the gods and goddesses sent out lights in the sky.

K—Kenaz, torch, illumination, warmth, awareness.

# 13. Backstage

BACKSTAGE IT WAS A SUNNY DAY. The hills in the distance brought unseen horizons to tickle the short soft grass underfoot. Two curtains hung on a tight line between two fantastic trees. The folds moved heavily in a breeze. The players watched the slight movement with some trepidation, much anticipation.

The curtains were backlit like a tapestry between two rooms, revealing the patterns of the Shakespeare monument. The slight waves of the folds rolled like a slow sea, flexing the stone pillars, the images of mythological deities, the typical sack of seeds, tied at the corners, used by the seed merchants of the day, with the obelisk arising between the carefully positioned arms of the Bard to spell out the runes for sun and moon, the seasons, the oracle, with further runes encoded in the alignments over the engraved words:

STAY PASSENGER, WHY GOEST THOU BY SO FAST?
READ IF THOU CANST . . .

The inscription continued, blending in and out of the light through the material.

The players had been informed that it was useless trying to go onstage just now. The trees would get in the way, or the curtains could not be moved enough. The information was incomplete, but they knew it was just as useless trying to force anymore information out of the messenger. They would become as involved as though he were one of the guardian trees. Or they would hear an incredible story. Or he would disappear. So they waited on the grass, backstage, under the open blue sky, under the stars.

They had been routinely involved in all the duties of putting on a show. But these familiar bustling achievements were slowing up in the general uncertainty and frustration. There was even a question of which play it would be. To pass the time, they had begun to trade parts and try out each other's roles. Competitive arguments simmered in some quarters, attracting the usual teasing to diffuse the tension.

A player who couldn't laugh at himself or herself was in trouble in more ways than he or she realized. This was backstage wisdom. They couldn't afford to let each other forget it. And it was a good excuse for some intense teasing. There was even more backstage wisdom about vicious behavior. Sometimes the wisdom was so obvious that players felt perfectly justified in administering it with force.

A broken player was a disaster. So the troupe was always on the alert to police the team spirit backstage and between shows generally.

Onstage, the words of the play were supposed to have enough cohesion to keep the personal egos of even the most hot-headed actors in abeyance by developing enough sense of direction and interest. If not, then either the playwright or the actor would have to go, peacefully as possible.

In the absence of the performance onstage, there had to be someone to continue the play, so to speak, until the next performance. This law enforcement officer had a variety of names, depending.

In view of his role in the interests of communication and harmony, some players called him Cupid. If they were trying to be ironic, they eventually discovered their mistake when just the right words brought them together with nothing but unmistakable love in the arms of their Harlequin or Columbine, somewhere backstage beneath immeasurable trees and stars.

This fooling around led to the name Harvey, famous for being a pooka, a Celtic hare on Broadway, sometimes a rabbit, otherwise known long ago as Puck.

This Easter Bunny made for a popular law enforcement officer. Although it was sometimes better if he was invisible. The idea was enough for the words. For him to appear like that was . . . sometimes too much. Unless he was wearing his English bobby's costume.

Most of the players were secretly relieved when he appeared in officer's uniform, instead of as an upstanding rabbit. Therefore they were rarely in a mood to call him Hermes without thinking it over first.

"Harvey" was more easy going and kept the balance of emotions at a tolerable level, as long as he looked human inside the uniform. It was then possible to speak logically, to stay on track, within the law, "if you know what I mean," a refrain that he used from time to time, like the swing of a baton. Most players called him PC, for Police Constable.

He had his own version of an East London accent, with inflections to enforce a grassroots understanding of the law. It was clear where he was comin' from; it was also a mystery. Mysteriously it was clear which way the mystery went, as long as you were with him, if you know what I mean.

People got all sorts of strange ideas about what he was about. They were discussing them now, backstage, trying to piece together which play it was going to be.

☙ ❧

On the other side of this puzzle, the four lovers were fragrant with the smoke of barbecued trout, the salad dressing, fruit and ice cream, their bodies rubbed and caressed with oils and fresh from the garden. They studied the image of the monument lit up onscreen in the lid of the art-box, plugged into a much larger screen.

They thought nothing of the fact that the inscription read the right way round in their direction as well, nor was it curious that there was no evidence of any curtain or of anyone behind or in front of it, except for the carefully posed image of Shakespeare.

Tanya was pointing out the runes. "You see that one?" It lit up with a rose-colored light under her touch. "Ansuz, the rune for the letter *A*. Now let's read," and she slowly read out the inscription at the base of the monument:

READ IF THOU CANST

"If you can read runes!—not: *if you can read this while reading this!* That would not only be redundant but silly, if not insulting. I mean, *read this, if you're illiterate*—seriously! But it turns out from my research that there's a tradition of runes being used playfully, often sending messages—with rune sticks, like the one archaeologists discovered that says, 'Kiss me.' But get this, lovers; it was not unusual for the runes to say something like, 'Interpret this if you can.' It was a challenge to solve a riddle. Or it was a way to engage students to learn a particular runic code. Like texting, but with an educational use as well. Runes were being used in the Middle Ages, and there is no reason why the

A—Ansuz, mouth, speech, inspiration, signals, gods, oracle.

living tradition couldn't have been known to a playwright of histories of ancient times. So check this out," and she indicated the lettering, even as the words lit up.

WHOM ENVIOUS DEATH HATH PLAST WITH IN THIS MONUMENT

She paused for effect and placed her finger on the next word.

SHAKSPEARE

"*Shakespeare*, meaning the plays. Read the plays, perchance? You can't read his body. And then we have this." The light seemed to come through her hand this time.

WHOSE NAME DOTH DECK Ys TOMBE

"There is no name on the tomb. It's clearly a riddle. Then there is the curse on the tomb itself, with its curious capitalization, for effect.

Good Friends for Iefus SAKE forbeare
To diGG T-E Duft Encloafed HERe
Blese be T-E Man Y/T fpares T-Hs Stones
And curst be He Y/T moves my bones.

"He really dose not want anyone checking on his whereabouts. Anyone hunting him back then, who decides to brass out the curse with a shovel; I mean, a real careful probe with a camera four centuries later tells us what they would have found—a body, headless—in a strangely shallow grave. Not there? So where's the infamous author of the Devil's word?"

"No positive ID, so they would have kept looking for him," pondered Julie. "On *deck*. Shakespeare on deck of—a tomb somewhere else? A ship to the Otherworld? Like the Norse tradition of shipping the dead off to the Otherworld in a burning boat on the water—with runes!"

"In a *tome*," said Lawrence.

"You mean tomb?" Jack tried to clarify.

"Wot I mean is, *tome*," Jack! "Given that this artist is not casually suspected of taking an interest in fonts an' such." He waited.

"Out with it, Lawrence!" said Julie. "Fonts?"

"Fonts an' etymologies, the look o' words. *Tomb* and the word, *tome*, a word for a weighty book? 'Ere we 'ave another play on words, do we not?" And he wiggled his ears convincingly. "Bard's puns?"

Tanya tried to be serious, not to lose the thread. "Plus, Lawrence, lover, you probably know that *tome* is related to the Latin *tomus*, a section of a larger book, a piece of paper or as in the Ancient Greek *témnō*, to cut or slice—*Shakespeare*, without putting too fine a point on it. His schooling in Latin and Ancient Greek would have given him plenty of wordplay, more than I got."

"Yet, the book you was workin' on 'as attracted more than a lit'le attention our way."

"Well," commented Jack, "if he was able to book on board a ship to a safe haven, we're going to have to come up with something a little more effective in a global transport economy. Don't see us just sailing away to Norumbega with your manuscript, Tanya."

"Well," she continued, "if he did *book* in 1616, the official date of his death, it was just in time. Anyone with a public profile like his was bound to get picked off by the Puritans sooner or later. And with his

Y—Jera, the rune for year, seasons, harvest, cycles, reincarnation.

sense of history, he wouldn't wait for the English Civil War to break out and the theater to be banned outright as the work of the Devil, in 1641. By then, Shakespeare would be seventy-eight years old, if he still lived. By 1616, actors had already been banned for the past decade from his hometown of Stratford. So he went about playing the merchant in grain and real estate, owning fields of grain himself. And again here's another hint to think outside the box."

LEAVES LIVING ART
BUT PAGE
TO SERVE HIS WITT

"Now I don't pretend to understand this whole thing, but it seems to me that you can sort of turn the page, as though the monument is a living book of his works. And guess who's the 'page' or servant there before you, mischievously coming alive, like Puck, pretending to be set in stone?—known to enjoy jokes and wordplay, puns and multiple meanings, like you say, Lawrence.

S—Sowilo, the sun, oracle, merging with community.

"And there we have the *Y* rune, Jera, for the harvest and the cycle of the seasons, which is being formed by combining the rune, Kenaz, for a source of illumination, like sun, moon or stars, or a torch!—" She touched it, and it lit up like sunlight. "With Isa, the rune for ice. Maybe too obvious as a simple vertical line."

In response, the line turned clockwise ninety degrees. Tanya caught her breath. "But add in Sowilo, the sun rune and the polarity within Eihwaz, the yew tree, famous for its kundalini, and, wow!—is that ice melting?"

The symbols glowed and merged with waves of colored light and drops of many hues that streamed down the buttoned-down, obelisk-like design, as from an icicle down the Bard's front or down a melting stalagmite rising from the sack of seeds, down and off-screen.

"Runes!" She exclaimed under her breath. "And you know these are more than just letters of an ancient pagan alphabet. Runes were designed to express the knowledge of the way words can channel nature. So they

Ei—Eihwaz, yew tree connecting life and death; Yggdrasil, tree of many worlds.

Z—Algiz, elk, communication with gods, defense.

are also symbols of nature.

"For example, the *A* rune—how do they light up by themselves, Jack?—represents the mouth as the 'source of divine utterance,' to quote one text. We're talking about oracles, sibyls, channeling.

"If these runes channel, the entire monument would be seen by Shakespeare as a kind of immortality, to use the literary trope, but something alive, a doorway between worlds, like a standing stone or a fairy hill or tumulus.

"It's just one of the many ways inspiration communicates between humans and the gods. And here comes Algiz!—the rune of the elk, the god Herne, the Green Man, a rune of communication with gods."

"Shakespeare was a pagan—is what you are saying, is it?" said Julie.

"Yes, I think he had more sense of kinship with the pagan world than with the twisted heretic-burning, cathedral-wrecking, science-hating, crusading of his own age and recent past, and before."

"An old-fashioned panpsychist? How's that for a word?" ventured Julie. "A newly minted word in Shakespeare's time, by the philosopher Francesco Patrizi, returning today in the philosophy of mind, to talk about the idea of landscapes with all the rocks, trees, hills and valleys and inhabitants, stones and all being alive and somehow participating in consciousness—like Lawrence's sensually aware landscapes."

"Paints, easel 'n canvass included," he quipped. "Though they's more asleep than the artist," he added quickly.

"I think the system is getting some clarity," remarked Jack with a smile.

"So," Tanya resumed, "Shakespeare was literally a Renaissance man, a humanist with a spiritual connection to pre-Christian myths and belief systems of antiquity. Plus, panpsychism was a popular perspective in his day. Take away the gods, goddesses, spirits, and sprites, and many of his plays would fall apart, many could never happen, no plot, nothing, same as the rest of his characters. The pagan deities are vital to his appeal, his charm. I can get so easily sucked into this monument and lost in the maze for the sheer fun of it, even though it just becomes my own fantasy within its structure of opportunities.

"For example, look for a play with Ansuz, the *A* rune, in the title, like *As You Like It*, with the character Rosalind, to paraphrase: the quintessence of every sprite? Heaven would in little show? That one body should be filled with all graces wide enlarged? In Greek mythology there were three graces: Aglaia or Brightness, Euphrosyne or Joyfulness, and Thalia in Bloom. Now listen to this!" And Tanya recited Orlando in the forest of Arden.

Hang there, my verse, in witness of my love:
And thou, thrice-crowned queen of night, survey
With thy chaste eye, from thy pale sphere above,
Thy huntress' name that my full life doth sway.
O Rosalind! these trees shall be my books
And in their barks my thoughts I'll character;
That every eye which in this forest looks
Shall see thy virtue witness'd every where.
Run, run, Orlando; carve on every tree
The fair, the chaste and unexpressive she.

"It's the moon, the goddess Artemis or Diana the huntress and Rosalind all mixed together by Orlando—and at a stretch, did the Bard know about the rune sticks? and runes on standing stones? You can see them today. He was sure to have known about tree spirits, fairies and goddesses as trees, shared by cultures the world over, usually feminine.

"So along comes Rosalind reading Orlando's words to Touchstone, like this.

From the east to western Ind,
No jewel is like Rosalind.
Her worth, being mounted on the wind,
Through all the world bears Rosalind.
All the pictures fairest lined
Are but black to Rosalind.
Let no fair be kept in mind
But the fair of Rosalind.

"He's comparing her to lines of pictures and words, and I just don't know where to stop.

"It's like Alonso says in *The Tempest* . . . what was it? Like . . . 'This is as strange a maze as ere men trod . . . Some oracle must rectify our knowledge.' On and on, play after play, the gods keep comin' to town."

"Well it stands to reason," Jack contributed, "that he would get the hell outta there. In addition, you have the whole background attack on the acting profession where they were all considered suspect by the Church as channels of demons and gods because they acted out other personalities. This relegated them to the lower classes, almost outcasts, if it weren't for their popularity, right? Now that I think about it, channeling was so widespread in the Temples and Churches that is was more a matter of competition—plus the fear of heresy, fear of the return of the old gods, fear of women."

"Shakespeare's women are real," said Julie. "Just as real as the men. Sometimes they are disguised as men, showing their equality. But the woman in a man's clothes is also the symbol of a channel. The voice of a male god could speak through a woman on stage. No wonder they outlawed women players! But that didn't stop us, especially outside London. Sometimes I feel like we were there. Look at that rune!" It had come to life with moving color.

"Ansuz again, for the mouth," Tanya continued. "It goes straight up through the Bard's mouth, the mouth in the helmet and the skull's mouth. And you see the little bird with its wings outspread as though it's singing, about to take flight? In heraldry, it's a falcon. But symbolically, in this context, I like to think it's also a robin, for Robin Goodfellow, on the hood of the helmet, a visual pun, if you like, for Puck and the channel in the hood, giving you Robin Hood. Folks had another name for Puck, remember—Robin Goodfellow. The slipstream connection, right there lined up in the rune for the oracle in living stone. Coincidence?

"Then for the diagonals, take one from the skull's mouth to the mouth of the nude figurine on the right, the other along the spear to the mouth of that other spirit on the right, life and death—repeated."

The rune moved, repeating itself in the monument in more alignments, in overlapping circles, leaving trails of colored light and lines radiating leys that developed a landscape in the background.

"How about *A Midsummer Night's Dream*," said Julie, "with Puck and Titania, Oberon and the fairy world? Obvious."

"Not forgetting the moth!" added Lawrence.

"The play within a play and the ass-man, Bottom?" pitched in Jack.

"Look at this," said Tanya, as she brought her finger up to the screen again. Another pattern lit up to join the lights and reached out to run along her finger, as her entire aura began to glow. She paused to look at her hand with its purple and pink pastels, like fur standing on end in a soft glow.

"The *M* rune in Midsummer," she continued. "Here we not only have the source of divine utterance, we have the gods themselves as characters in a comedy that delves into the human soul. The soul is represented by the rune for *M*, Mannaz.

"The runes combine sound with images of entire ideas while making up words. This one's mapped out along the two straight pillars of the stage, and its diagonals at the top cross at the Bard's forehead, the place where the soul sees out of the astral body, the third eye.

"The diagonals start midway down the pillars, for midsummer, right? Then, after they cross at the third eye of the man, they connect with the pillars on the opposite sides, completing the rune in the third eyes of the two cat deities positioned on top of the pillars! The human and astral worlds merge with nature."

"This is a dream," said Jack.

"This is not random, lovers. This is by design. And I do believe, it's more than human design. The gods guided this sculpture. Mannnaz is also the rune for interdependence and helping each other. It's

M—Mannaz, humankind, soul.

the worlds coming together, just as in *A Midsummer Night's Dream* the human world, including the animal world, works out in the play because of the way the gods show up in the maze. This monument is a maze that opens up and can guide us. It's more than just a riddle, because its alignments have been inspired by more than just humans. It's like the data crystal. It's living art, referred to in the inscription. And that rune there, Ingwaz, shaped by the Bard's curiously poised arms either side of the obelisk arising from the sac of seeds? It's literally the rune for the sac of seeds of a fertility god, the scrotum of the totem pole! The Greeks might have called this a Herm, the phallic monuments women would caress along the roadsides?—to be with Hermes? Puck? Read if thou canst, whom!"

" 'Whom envious death hath placed within this monument.' No dead body of the Bard in the stone monument itself, obviously," said Julie. "Leaving the runic references there to read, if you can. As for Envious Death, who's that? We're talking major personification. Like, we've got Envious Death pursuing us, okay? Panpsychism precludes death, except as another side of life. Maybe it's just our present circumstances, but I feel a sense of urgency in common with the Bard being forced to sail away. But here we are, so maybe we've already

Ng—Ingwaz, the fertility god, whose runic symbol represents the seed bag, journey over land and water.

come home to live up to the pressures together, none of us having to be him.

" 'Whose name doth deck his tomb': no name on Shakespeare's supposed tomb in the church floor. Except the reference to Jesus in the curse on the nameless tomb—Jesus, whose tomb, as we all know, was found empty, a trail of dust, if the story of his escape is to be believed."

"An' what about that word, 'quick'? It says, 'with whom quick nature died. Another play on words? Why quick?" Lawrence enquired.

"Quick like Hermes?" asked Julie. "Quick nature? A redundancy by Shakespeare? Unless quick of wit. Quick as in alive, like the immortal gods and goddesses in the runes? Not really dead. Pan, sometimes, is said to live in a cave where the river Alpheus bubbles up as the Underground Stream in myth; something these churches like to usurp caves. Pan is described with phallic symbols in art. His name of course means 'all.' Kind of ironic in the church and the concept of no name and no body in the temple of the All-in-All and the one God and everything, and Pan's in Arcadia and Arcadia is . . ." she hesitated, "Norumbega? The State of Maine? Quick as the Running Christ?"

"Well that church is fast becoming a pantheon, if you ask me," said Jack. "And you're channeling something, to be sure—"

"Someone!" corrected Tanya with a laugh.

"Ever hear of that fat knight, Sir John Falstaff and Mistress Quickly? Does the Bard look like he's indicating fatness to you, Jack?" and Tanya tickled him. "That whole play. Anyway, talk about Ramesses and the gods and goddesses comin' to town! Well, puttin' this monument in a church sort of had a leveling effect on God. The one and only became one of the many—like Falstaff."

"Fair's fair," said Lawrence, "seeing's 'ow most of them churches is sittin' on stone circles and pagan temples, anyways; I mean it's only natural in the process of time for them to revert, in a forward sense, if you know wot I mean."

"Meaning, for example," said Tanya, "the image of the man in the funerary monument in the Stratford church today is not this one we have here. This one was carefully engraved by Wenceslaus Hollar. And Lawrence, you know, oooo I mean! He didn't mess around. Furthermore, it was crafted with the guidance of the Bard's granddaughter, Elizabeth Barnard and Sir William Dugdale, the scholar and historian, who popped it into his book, *Antiquities of Warwickshire*. It stands out there as one amazingly precise and of course accurate illustration.

This is how Shakespeare wanted the church monument to be. Of course, that would never stand back then, what with the English Civil War an' all. It was eventually, um, remodeled—despoiled by the victors?—to look like, I'd say, a sturdy Roundhead or a Puritan, in an Oxford University undergraduate's garb? Seriously?— I mean if you read or watch some of the plays and have a look at the current monument, you can imagine how horrified the guy would be to be portrayed like that caricature. A palpably pompous ass with quill pen writing on, would you believe, a sheet of paper on a pillow. Ever tried to write on a cushion? I have. Is this some inside joke? Everybody knew Oxford shunned Shakespeare. And have him suited up as an undergraduate, belittling him. Say no more."

"It's in the runes," said Lawrence. "And observe the intentionality of the way the arms are purposefully presented in a kind of self-consciously meditational pose, with them seed-like buttons. 'From the east to western Ind, no jewel is like Rosalind'? There's something to meditate on, Tanya!"

They watched the interplay of changes in the image for a while, as the Buddha-like Bard turned into a variety of other characters.

Tanya wondered aloud, "What about Ann Page and her family? Like it says in *The Merry Wives of Windsor.* There's so much to say about all this. So, now that it's here in the system, Jack, all I can think of is . . . the maze." She kissed him lightly on the rim of the ear, and in a stage whisper, "Thank you." Then she added: "Jack, how does it do all that? I mean, how does it know?"

"That should be me thanking you, Dark Lady, for all the research. It's a puzzler . . . has more pieces than we do. Lots of information . . . but there's more to it than that. It communicates to the point where it puts you in touch, not just with a piece of the truth, but the truth itself somehow, and that turns out to be more than just information. It turns out to be love. But you know that. So it ends up communicating between souls, putting them in touch with each other. The true polarity is love—love of *one another. Of the other.* Not just sexual polarity. So obvious!" He put his face in his hands.

"It—" said Julie flatly. "The data crystal fails to love, of course."

They sat in silence for a while.

"We still have to clear that data crystal," said Tanya finally.

"Credibili'y," added Lawrence mischievously.

They looked at Tanya, who was just staring into the screen. "Well," she offered, "it's caught up with everything we've been saying, *lovers* . . . and doing—so it's redundant for anyone to go and try and convince it that Jesus is just Jesus . . . so . . . I don't know what to say . . . or expect, quite frankly."

"How do we know it's not clear already?—" Julie said it like a statement that slipped out.

"It hasn't told us it believes us!" said Lawrence with some frustration.

"You mean it hasn't confirmed what we believe is true," clarified Julie.

"Correct."

"Would we believe it?"

" 'Ave we asked it?"

"I'm not sure," said Tanya. "Has anyone wondered . . . I mean, if you know what I mean—about polarities?"

"Have we?" asked Jack, "I now know I was wrong, but can it love?"

Having remained still for some time in their silence, the image of Shakespeare moved, as though relaxing from holding words in position. He stretched out his arms, and the runes for woman, fertility, the moon, and new beginnings filled with starlight. A full moon arose within the gesture and expanded to fill the stage, eclipsing the Bard and the sack of seeds at the base of the obelisk. The moon darkened as a corona began to shine around the clearly defined rim.

The radiance around the ring of sunlight intensified outwards until it rippled into seeds, as though the mundane sack had been opened at the center of his soul merged with the sun. The eclipse moved back, and the stage opened out into the distance, while the pillars became trees on either side, plowed fields beyond. The seeds sailed over the fields and settled into furrows.

Then they heard through the speakers the voice of a woman sing a rune for the seasons. Rain fell, and she sang a rune for the sun. The seeds reappeared as fields of barley, full grown, ready for harvest.

A crop symbol appeared. The fields returned to the stage as a tapestry between the trees, with the sun's aura shining through the patterns of barley woven this way and that.

Jack recognized the symbol as the one he had seen formed with Bellarose, Jesús and John. The one he had not been confident enough to install into the data crystal inside the art-box, back at the trailer.

The symbol in the tapestry turned into a maze of more colored lights moving harmoniously in opposite directions. It filled the room with its brilliance, radiating from liquid streams like molten glass beads over the walls, the ceiling, the floor, slipping along their naked bodies.

They heard a cockney accent in parody of itself: " 'Ello, 'ello, 'ello! If, you know wot I mean!" They laughed, Lawrence's eyes widened.

"How d'ya credit that one?" Jack enquired.

They could see their auras glowing and merging in the continuous rainbowed beads of light.

"Our crystal definitely looks all clear to me," said Lawrence. "Not that I'm a scientist, mind you. But as an artist of sorts, it looks quite clear, quite clear, all right." His eyes carefully followed some of the lights in their circular currents throughout the room, taking mental notes along the way. He looked at his hands, the way the aura radiated through layers, intensely but softly, out and out, wider layers radiating into wider overlapping translucent layers, sensing the atmosphere with his entire being, out beyond the room and into the night, realizing that it was filled with the same light, into space.

The sun and moon, the stars, planets and galaxies no longer seemed separated by physical distance so much as by time, the time that had passed since he had known some of them intimately and had forgotten. The personal experience of another world was more important than its physical distance. He felt his senses could touch it, or he could ride out there once more, now that he felt the location personally: a reunion was possible. But he couldn't recall anymore about it. The potential had opened up, nothing more.

Then he remembered the eclipse: it was all about having a mission on earth. He wondered what the others were thinking. He felt immense love. They all felt it. It was who they were and who was already with them, reunited always.

The lights quickly flowed back into the wide, invisible atmosphere whence they had emerged. The bands of colored auras were likewise returned into the wider truth, as the lovers' perceptions focused on the next step along the way.

"Now all we've got to do is clear the main system," said Jack, sounding oddly technical.

"But we don't know how we did this!" said Julie. "So how can we do that? And we're still taking this as proof that the backdoor crystal here in the art-box is clear. Lawrence?"

He took her in his arms, "You're right, we're not there yet, are we now?"

"It's got to identify him for us," said Tanya, "hasn't it, Jack?"

The monument was back on screen, solid as stone. A camera moved in closer, bringing them the stage.

"Who's got that camera, I wonder," said Julie.

"Always wondered that myself," Jack replied. "We used to call it the 'slipstream camera.' It got to be so contentious no one mentioned it anymore."

The image of the Bard became textured once again and drew apart, unbuttoned along the obelisk, like two curtains. Beyond there was a beach with the ocean. They could hear the seductive waves. They waited, becoming an audience.

Backstage, the curtains had finally lifted, parted, but the players, to their consternation, were also becoming an audience, contrary to expectations. They were soothed to some extent by the sound of the waves as well, mixing with their pleasure at discovering themselves by the beach on that sunny day beneath the stars.

I — Isa, ice.

# 14. Tales of the Running Christ

It was the autumnal equinox, long awaited, when the television sets and monitors, phones and devices of choice were tuned to the same station. Few could imagine how anyone but those severely caught out of luck could not be watching at this time in history. The event was being compared with the first moon landing by the Apollo 11 mission. It was being stated as the next logical step for man.

The audiences gathered in sports stadiums filled with holograms and rows of giant screens, in cinemas, town squares, parks and at home, staring into the peaceful waves on the beach, out to the horizon, an ocean of eyes expecting an eye in the ocean, a vision, personal to each, universal, to connect them once and for all, to solve them each one, as promised.

Just about everyone who had access in the world was there. Who could resist just having a look when so many were so sucked in? And what reasonable person would stand against the organization of such a worldwide performance when there was so much truth behind it, evidenced by the incredible strides in communications technology?

NASA was on the defensive; their ways appeared slow and overly mechanical, almost Victorian, by comparison to what was happening in this world of invisible messengers bringing entire worlds together at the speed of light, and faster, if illusions were not what we had thought. Whose light, whose illusion was it?

For a year and more they had experienced it personally, hearing it from friends and family, from colleagues and co-workers, or directly on screen, as it gathered all their previous experience into focus in the cybercult. Strong allegiances to one or more of the six cybertypes had been forged in the *Orpheus Chronicles*. Thus the types were systematically being "freed" from the typifications that had imprisoned them, the greatest prison guard of them all being the Bard of Stratford.

No one in their right mind would deny that something profound was happening. It would be irresponsible for the concerned citizen to turn away and not watch the thing unfold. For this was billed as nothing less than the raising of an enclosed city: the lost Atlantis! sunk in the Bermuda Triangle, invisibly imprisoned in a recently discovered interplanetary energy, known by the media cult as the Slipstream.

Bellarose, Samantha, Jesús and John watched the horizon, joined in the vast audience.

Bellarose said, "You'd never think all those nuts and bolts you were describing have been working away in and around that monitor all this time, would you? All they do is turn to the channel and the system plugs back into their cybertypes through the slipstream; off they go together, building the cult.

"I guess it's been happening all through history, in communications, ritual, theater, in language, for that matter, like an undetected telepathy. It's just that now they can get the system to automatically fine tune the show for the types as they watch. I've heard of people just getting so into it they just watch the same image for hours at a time, calling it meditation or worship, a religious experience."

"It's simply that you've got no well-defined cybertype for the system to access," said Jesús. "It didn't affect you the way it does the others. For you, it's just boring."

"So we just never watched," said Sam.

Jesús eyed her and scratched his chin. "You didn't? Huh, curious . . . Why not?"

"Haven't you heard these people talk about their cult soaps? 'Chronicles,' they call them! You think I'd be into that?" She looked back and flashed her eyes at him. "I suppose you would!"

He giggled and blushed, "Would what?"

She exhaled with frustration, looked up at the beams in the ceiling and back to the screen, then slumped further into the beanbag on the Persian carpet over the old farmhouse floorboards. "I'm not going to like this," she added.

There was a pause in the New Age elevator music that had been mixed with an enhanced crashing and lapping of waves. The voice of one of the Project's most famous news anchors spoke in his usual friendly affirmative monotone intended to signify factual reports: "Before we begin, Project Light Center would like to request a moment of silence. The world is learning of the recent loss of our

Secretary General, Jesús de l'Orient, Sr., who suffered a heart attack at the Château de Solion, while preparing today's historic event. Sadly, he will never witness it as he would have wished. Let us therefore join in a moment of silent prayer and remembrance."

Jesús simply said, "I know, it's OK. We saw him, remember?"

They waited.

The voice quickly returned, leaving as little dead air as possible. "It is often said that the great things in life cannot happen without great loss. Let us therefore turn to this truly momentous event. Soon we will hear from the voices that have touched us all so deeply this past year. But first, just to assure you that what you are about to witness over the electronic media is in fact happening, we will turn to one of our correspondents aboard one of the many Air Force and civilian jets that are now flying out there over the Atlantic Ocean. Over to you, Barbara!"

"Typical A3 lead-in," commented Jesús, "not bad, huh?" He looked up playfully from the floor where he was seated, Indian style.

Barbara took over, "Thank you, Ralph! Hello world! It's difficult to exaggerate the high emotion in this aircraft as we circle the waves far below in the dark, waiting for any sign. And yet, nothing, Ralph, nothing at all, yet."

They engaged in a brief repartee intended to demonstrate that this was reality, happening, confirmed and brought to you, the viewer, as is, you, as defined, the viewer.

"Barbara's another A3," Jesús added, "through and through."

The other three tensed up but decided to let it pass. They relaxed in the unspoken excuse that he was a scientist, he'd built the system, he was now watching it in action. It would be strange if he weren't totally involved in the components, especially if those puzzle pieces were totally involved somehow in him.

Maybe, after all, he wasn't jumping to conclusions. Maybe he really could identify people so thoroughly and quickly by now. They hesitated and began to watch him unobtrusively as he watch the screen.

The three of them discovered each other glancing at the way he was so engrossed in an event that consisted mainly of invisible expectation, filled to brimming with symbols and emotions already featured in the Chronicles.

John ventured to put his hand in the air over his head, palm upwards as Jesús had done by the stones, feeling the cybernet, the cult. His hand tingled.

"Feel it?" said Jesús, smiling like a cherub.

"Yep. It activates a tingling response in my hand and a slight physical pressure, like it's an electrically charged fluid medium, slightly more dense than air."

Jesús was focused back into the screen.

Clouds rolled into view. They curled round into a circle until they were no longer clouds, but more like smoke and fire cycling round an empty center where flames stretched out from the inner rim to encircle the wheel like claws all round turning black as they gripped the fire, as though making it spin faster and holding on increasingly as it did so.

It began to look molten and solid, as though it were melting at extreme temperatures. It turned white with red claws that began to drip like blood, as though it were now ice being gripped until it bled with emotion. It pulsated and burst into clouds once more, then into flame, wheeling all the while.

"Don't worry," said Jesús, "it's just the cybercult, special effects. Means nothing, really."

"Barbara!"

"Yes, Ralph?"

"Do you see anything?"

"It's all in the system so far . . . nothing visible over the Atlantic. No reports of anything, nothing at all! Isn't this wonderful!"

The center of the wheel opened, revealing an eye with a round pupil. It looked from side to side and then remained fixed in the center. The claws became eyelashes, and the wheel stood still. Then it squeezed down heavily to become oval, eye-shaped, shedding a few drops of red fire from one corner.

A voice accompanied it through the speakers into every ear, in the languages of the people in attendance throughout the world. "This technology has brought us to the threshold of our journey. You chroniclers of Orpheus will recognize me from the episodes that we have created together. Now we are here!"

"Cybertype A2," said Jesús, mesmerized in a stage whisper.

The eye seemed to twitch slightly in response. The voice continued. "Together we have created, each one of you, with the system, episodes that we have called the *Orpheus Chronicles*! I ask you now, now that the year is past, who is this Orpheus we have chronicled in our personal journeys in the cybercult together? Who is Orpheus? Who is this man? If he is a man— The time has come to find him out.

"This myth is real. Because the cult is unashamedly the truth! It comes to you in your dreams. This technology has made those dreams enter the daylight hours. As I speak, we bring the power of the cult to bear. We find out the truth behind our personal hopes and ancient primordial desires, and we bring the dawn in the ocean, and we raise the ship of the sun!

"We discover this man, Orpheus of legend. We find him standing before the gods of Olympus. Not as the man of myth and legend but in our own fantasies and dreams where we have looked into the glass to find ourselves looking back, Orpheus—not just a man but a force.

"Not just a woman, sitting at home before her television in the middle of her day in the middle of her life, lost and looking, no! A force! Orpheus!

"Man and woman, one force before Mount Olympus, before the gods! A force to be reckoned with, a demanding power that they cannot deny. This power makes one statement: 'You have stolen my love!'

"The gods are on the defensive.

"The force repeats: 'Your brother, the King of the Underworld has stolen her! Let me pass! You have no right to divide the power of love!'

"Chroniclers! You have dreamed from episode to episode in the cult, each one of you, that you will be reunited! You have all spoken that it is your right. You should not be divided from your love. You have the power. You have the right! You are right in this!

"Now dream with me! Feel the power with me! Orpheus!

"But the gods tell him, 'But your love, it has been bitten by a snake!' They sidetrack him with a snake! An excuse! Two worlds separated by nothing more than a snake?

"You have all been held back from your dreams. By nothing more than a snake. Snakes and rats are given to you as explanations, nothing more! Snakes and rats!

"And now your families are broken. Snakes and rats? Is this enough to break the bonds of a family brought together by the bonds of love and blood? You dream of a new family, as it was, before the underworld and the gods.

"Now you demand reunion, communion in the family of your dreams! You cannot be denied.

"The gods give in. Gods have no authority over love. Orpheus is given safe passage to the Underworld to find Eurydice, his love, his wife.

"This is what is happening to us all at this moment. Witness! The door to the Underworld is about to open!"

Some dramatic music took over from the voice.

"Ralph, we're witnessing it! Yes . . . there's something . . . I don't know whether we can get it on camera . . ."

"I think, Barbara, we have an image from one of our satellites. There! We've inserted it on screen for our viewers, in a box. No, sorry, the eye's in the box.

"Now the overview of the Atlantic is on the main screen. Yes, we see it, thank you Barbara! A kind of cloud formation. A weather system in the dark—most unusual. Vast, from Africa to America. Filled with colored lights! They are moving in formation. Incredible speed, Barbara. A triangle! They have mapped out the triangle from Bermuda to Puerto Rico . . . to— They're circling round now. It's a circle of lights! They're flying in opposite directions in concentric rings in the dark, lighting up the clouds."

The music receded while the inserted box expanded to return the eye to its previous position in the center of the screen. The beach was gone, and now the eye advanced until the pupil blacked out the scene. The voice continued: "Witness the Underworld, O Orpheus! You, the force, separated in blackness!

"Now you stand before the King and Queen of Death. You must perform! They must be persuaded! More gods to appease! And who is this Persephone?

"She is a queen, and she claims to be abducted by her king? She goes home to her mother, who you may call Demeter, once a year? She surfaces from her marriage in the spring, and we have the sad complaint?

"All you women who are married to your kings and masters! We understand! You are credited! Therefore, men! Husbands! Masters! Credit her! Understand her!

"Witness your credits! The gods dance to your tune!"

The colored lights circled in the darkness within the pupil of the eye.

"Good, good, more! Very good. Orpheus can persuade, his music is very persuasive, Persephone dances round and round, they all dance."

The music played louder and faster with the dancing lights.

"Persephone, like the rest, falls for his music. As long as he has what it takes to hang in there! Credit him! Don't let him waver! He's the actor of the moment. He must not let fall his mask; that's his thing right now: his mask of music. In the dark Underworld. He needs all the credits you can give so he can reunite with his love, so we can reunite!

"Women and wives! What do you say to your mothers about your men? You say they are not faithful! You say they are! You say they might be either faithful or unfaithful! You say that that's their thing! The men! So credit them now! Understand them! It's their way! Come together in the force, for the force is love! Hear Orpheus play! Credit him!

"Now the gods of the Underworld, we call them Hades and Persephone—there are as many names as we have names—people of the cybercult, people who are with us in the Project Light Center, listen! The gods listen to the music, its power, and they impose a condition.

"The man of the house, the king in his castle, he lives in a place of mystery and darkness to the ones outside his family. He is king of his own Underworld, where it is his lantern that shows his truth, something in the blood. A darkness that is light! A family reason. He imposes a condition; the queen agrees with her king.

"The Gods of Olympus, the wider family, they all impose conditions on love. Credit the family! It's their thing, the program! The family! Understand it! I hear your credits comin' in!"

The music came faster, tailored to each ear, and the lights flew in opposite circles against the dark background. "Good! Now I want to feel those credits as we have never felt them before!

"What does the myth say the condition was? What was the mythological condition on love, what made it so real that we understand it to this very day and we credit it in the cult? We give it power! What was it? Give it voice! I hear some of you now. I hear your hearts ring out, and I am hearing your voices start the world over! I hear you say it in more and more numbers. I hear you say . . . the conditional words that come in waves bringing love! The love that is carried on the conditions imposed by love! Freely, I say it with you . . . we say it together! Don't look back! Don't look back! It's their thing, so don't look back! Don't look back! No, don't look back, people, don't look back! Feel the cult and understand it with your credits, all your credits now give them over, now, all of them and don't look back! Don't think how often we say it, now . . . don't even think it because you don't look back to when we said it last, we don't look back because we are entering the threshold and we move into the future, we don't look back so we have the power! The power that is bringing us all together in the eternal moment."

"Ralph! Ralph!"

"Barbara!"

"Ralph! I don't know how to describe it! Ralph, it's so wonderful!"

"Don't look back, Barbara, don't look back!"

"Don't look back, Ralph! Don't look back!"

They entered into the chant as the system released the voices in their many languages like waves breaking with the words together, foaming at the mouth.

Jesús was clutching his knees, resisting the pull of the cult that pulled on his armor, tugging, cajoling and threatening every scale and ring of it with the madness to enter the chant, to drop the mask and enter the chant, the forbidden communion. It was eating away at his panoply. The pressure was pulling him apart. He was too much like them.

It was forbidden to him, Jesús, the provider, to partake.

The power was divided. Increasingly it was being called away just to keep him together with his monumentally subtle mask, his panoply of costumes for every conceivable occasion with every variation on all the types of the cult, not to mention the intimate transactions with creative souls on the slipstream, and the gods, the goddesses!

The voice cut in with the promise of a rescue: "She follows him! She arises from within the ocean, from the world within the ocean, to the world above the ocean, out of the darkness of the unseen family of angels into the light of your vision where you can see the creditworthy ship of Atlantis, named *Eurydice!* Out of the darkness of her home she rises in communion with the family of man!

"Credit her! People of the Orphic force, keep the faith, don't let it slip, he keeps the mask and we come together!"

Jesús felt it slipping away from him. He began to sway from side to side.

The intensity of the oceanic roar of voices in the speakers slackened.

"He weakens!" the voice cried to the people. "Orpheus weakens! He is losing the mask of music and power!"

Jesús stiffened. He smiled feebly round the room and looked back into the big monitor. The music was completely overtaken by millions of voices that surged with renewed resolve in languages from round the world. They cheered him on.

Again, he wanted to join them. He was not who they thought he was! He was a man of the twenty-first century. He had survived the sexual revolution. When had he ever been what they thought or dreamed? It was all an act!

They had to keep the faith. They had their masks. But they were dead wrong about him. The reality was different from their masks. It did not fit the act anymore. So they had to make it fit. They were calling for all they were worth, and their masks were falling away. Many were in shreds, trampled underfoot. They were saving him by giving away their soul credits, risking all against nature, while throwing in their armor of cybertypes, gambling on the success of the event that promised all.

They had looked out at the world through masks of precious, powerful materials that provided them with cover and projected images in the minds of others. Now they placed their bets on him.

They were addicted, some more than others. They were sure that the return would be worth the investment in him. They had no idea what they were doing or who he was. They had always been like this, for so long!

They were saying something crazy for him, blinding themselves with the words, putting all faith in him with those words that they were chanting: Don't look back, don't look back!

His armor was peeling off. It was old. He was tired. The pressure to be someone undefined was escalating. A nobody? Their credit was not enough. Who were they? He didn't know who he was or what he should do. He wanted to join them and chant: Don't look back, don't look back. They were breaking down together.

They needed new words and new parts in the play. But it was as though everything had been tried, for two thousand years and more, thousands of years more in the wider cult, before Serapis, back to Atlantis and beyond to other planets.

The voice called once more: "Save him! More credit! Save him! He is Orpheus the world over. People everywhere, save him. Only you have the credit to save the Christ, Orpheus! The Orphic Christ force in us all. Sing out for the ship! Don't look back! Don't look back!

"There are no laws to stop you now! You have the credit to do it now. Save him! Act! Act now!"

The sound of the chanting voices subsided in a questioning vacuum that felt as though it could suck anything into the unknown depths. The room thickened up.

"No need to test the vibes," declared Bellarose.

She looked at Sam who was wide-eyed, as though with a thought that she was about to share. Before anyone had a chance to ask, she came out with it: "It's the myth of the Running Christ, the pre-Christian running man!"

"What's that?" said John.

She smiled mysteriously: "Run, run, run? Just as fast as you can?—"

"Can't catch me, I'm the Gingerbread Man!" he chimed in. "Fox, he gets him, no?"

"He tries to cross a river," said Bellarose. "Thinks he can control the fox, climbs on fox's nose."

"Gets eaten," Sam confirmed.

"*Everybody* likes the Gingerbread Man! Yummy!" John exclaimed.

"Old heretical tale from the Cathar days, if not before," Sam continued. "Native Americans have Running Christ tales also. We put him with his brother, the twin, sometimes. In Jerusalem, the twin gets crucified; the other identical twin, he runs. The fox gets him back in the gingerbread heresy.

"Native Americans sometimes have him teamed up with the fox . . . or coyote . . . or wolf. He's the raven or the hawk . . . like Horus, the Egyptian Pharaoh? Different tribes, different versions. But the tales are so ancient, who knows, eh?

"This Jesus was a Pharaoh, maybe. What did you say, John? And he ran through the Americas more than one lifetime?" She laughed, "Looking for Mary or maybe Roxanne?"

There was no reply. John was admiring her instinctive response to some outlandish hints he had made to test the possibility of telling his story of riding down the slipstream, of remembering Ptolemy. It was so natural an occurrence, but he was still wondering when and how to tell it in this world. She was always surprising him with the edges of his own ideas as these waited on the surface of his mind. He looked into her eyes gently, waiting for more.

"Can't we turn that thing off!" she exclaimed in the direction of the TV.

Jesús was swaying gently, unable to hear her, engrossed in the babbling multitude welling up once more.

She moved to pick up the remote. He wheeled with rage in his eyes. The chanting leveled off, losing the diverted energy. She froze. He snatched it and used it to regain control. He turned up the sound. The chanting returned with a roar, augmenting the sound even further.

She lapsed back into the beanbag and rolled her eyes. "He runs but he doesn't really know why," she called above the growing din. "It's a wheel going nowhere. No infinity, no future, a wheel that is absurd, that stops all the time to pump itself up! It fascinates the Indians, so they attach all these stories to learn from human nature. It's a program.

"He says they're after him. He looks for help from nature. He looks for someone to slay his dragons. That's you, John!

"He runs back to the Temple that has sent out the pursuers. They are out of control. He harnesses them with nature's help in the form of the dragon slayers. He gets in trouble in connection with them, looking for credit, to be a Lancelot! He picks up the medals for his armor, he strikes new poses, chastises the Temple and returns to his divine throne, in the Temple itself!

"He is like a circus master above gods and demons who do tricks for him. He has performed another sacrifice, his friendship, his love, he sacrifices nature and the Temple is pumped up. Soon, the demons are out of control once more. Off he runs again, looking for help—a dragon slayer, a nature spirit god, a soul, help! He threatens disaster among the innocents. Innocent people will get hurt if the gods don't respond! It's the hostage program. But always he has to look as though he is helping them. It's the running man.

"All the stories are told by the people who see him pass. Indians see him run by. He is tense and secretive. They see him stop and ask for a favor. But he performs a miracle to make it look like he is giving them the favor, instead. Always has to be the great provider, even when he is tattered and torn.

"His secrecy builds tension. It's the Temple. Dark and secret.

"For example, he stops in front of the recently sewn field. He makes the seeds grow suddenly into a crop ready for harvest."

"With a little help from nature!" shouted John.

Her eyes flashed in reply. "He then tells the farmer to tell the pursuers that he ran by when the seeds were sewn. He tells him to lie; it's their little secret between the two of them; he sort of initiates the farmer into a bit of the cult; then he runs. Maybe the farmer will get the sickness, and he will run. What can he do? The farmer is supposed to make the temple's demons assume the running man is way ahead of them. The farmer is sucked in. He tells the wrong story. More secrets, more lies. He behaves like the trickster. The trickster himself has got his energy and becomes more like a god. With each story he becomes the Running Christ!

"The secrets build up the tension, the tension needs a release. He sacrifices nature, people of color, Indians, Jews, other Christians, anyone in the end! Himself!

"Because, you see, he's just in the program like all the rest. History has given him a crown, but he's just a man. Everyone in society who has a mask wants to make sure *his* mask stays in place. Society depends on it! So much illusion, theater! Society collapses, they forgot who they are. They don't ask. They collapse, like now.

"The Indians watch. The stories are amusing. Little did they know, at first, what this amusing perspective would cost them."

"So what did the farmer get out of it?" shouted Bellarose, "A story, a myth?"

"Some stories will run longer than the Christ and say more about him than we know. In some versions he's called Quetzalcoatl, the feathered serpent! The Aztec should know. They were sacrificing hundreds of people a year by the time the Christians sacrificed them. Same program, different ways. The Aztec was more formal, made the Christians look like savages."

"Looking for a dragon slayer!" said John. Then he leaned over and shouted in Jesús's ear: "Hey, man, ya gotta stop!"

The Christ turned and smiled playfully. Then, with an offhand snap of the wrist, he brought the sound back down. The crowds of voices surged again into a renewed roar at lower volume: surge upon quiet surge of "Don't look back, don't look back! Orpheus, don't look back!" He had resumed control. He tossed the remote aside, a small miracle of technology.

Sam finished her tale: "The raven—he's sometimes called the trickster—he and his twin, they're exceptional, they go down into the Underworld to bring back their wives. It's the same basic story on both sides of the Atlantic, intended to block the knowledge of reincarnation.

"The twins look back and lose their wives forever to death in the underworld, of course.

"Some Native Americans say that this is the story of why, of all the living spirits in nature that cycle back to life in reincarnation, only humans die forever and don't come back. People are special. And the chief will always be a chief!

"Often they would warn the audience before they tell the story: This is the story of why *some* people think we are all so superior! It is often a question of how the story is told.

"In my opinion, this Orpheus myth is another running man tale that has been twisted. He runs to the gods with his problem. They make an exception. He goes down into death to return, but hey, what's this at the last? He screws up, poor lover, self destructs a little.

"He's *resurrected* from the Underworld, having blown it. No reincarnation! No thank you. Not this time!

"Soooo, too bad about the wife. Typical male. The entire program depends on the suppression of the female.

"If women live through death, then it's curtains, macho-male program, bye-bye! And oh my, how he loved her, oh yes, my dear! He thinks he'll keep her, but—oops, too bad. Back she goes.

"Trickster is always the traitor.

"He's just a man to the Indians. So there are plenty of spin-off running men.

"Can't you just see the sad look on his face? Oh poor Romeo! Well, it's back to Rosie or Carolyn, the one he left before. Finally he's been too clever and fox gets him, eats him. It's a tragedy, certainly not a religion!" She gave Jesús an infuriated look and brushed the bright black hair away from her face. If he knew about being with a woman, then he would know nature and love!—end program.

"Where is he going all the time, running, just running to nowhere? No direction. For the Indians of North and South America, he just runs, and that's the interest where the tales are generated.

"There is only one tale of how they get him and it was not often told. Only one tale out of many, not interesting. He never gets reincarnated, but he just keeps on going. His immortality is in myth. Indians and heretics told the tales of the Running Christ. He gave us nothing but death and destruction. It's a program. It runs on, blaming everything on skin color, country of origin, the Spanish or the white man!

"The Native Americans have been here for many thousands of years. *His* stories are short and they run in circles, going nowhere, unless you can learn from the folly. Yet it wears the mask of eternity.

"He is faceless unless he recognizes the hell inflicted on the people in the attempt to wipe out the American past! He must know the past to survive it. He must navigate by looking back."

"Is that why they call it dead reckoning?" John enquired with a straight face.

"Why do I get the feeling you guys are talking about me behind my back?" Jesús tried to look like he was into it.

"We are," said John. "I guess it's time we moved into the mainstream, Jesús."

"Mainstream?" the Christ went pale and the roar died away in the speakers, the dancing lights vanished into the darkness.

Then the screen blushed with rage, while he tried to remain impassive, while they tried to save him, each in his or her own private tale of the Running Christ, wheeling in the cybercult, foaming at the mouth, chanting, "Don't look back!"

O—Othila, legacy, heritage.

# 15. Indecision

The Indian, whom Jesús had called Uncle Sam, had figuratively pulled the rug out from under him where he sat in front of the wide screen. It was a light touch by one member of a people who had suffered the loss of a fifth of the world's population in contact with the Christians from the arrival of Columbus to the present day. After that, who would look back? The cybertypes were shouting their heads off now: "Don't look back!"

Jesús wanted to join them all the more. It would be a way out. He was becoming helplessly racist towards Sam.

She was undoing him. All those credits were worthless when it came down to her research, her knowledge and logic and the fact that she cared.

He watched his credit money burn in the dancing lights.

There was evidence in those wild colored lights that she did, in fact, care, as though saying, "I care nothing for your money, your social credit, nothing! I care about you. I love you. I'm glad your credit burns!"

He denied that she gave a damn about him. Her love was undressing him, while underneath it all, he wanted to make love in his armor.

Bellarose and John had met him gently in his soul, not asking him to disarm. It hadn't been an issue with them. They just let him be himself for once, armor and all. So his soul had escaped the armor and run free in a crop circle, in nature, feeling unconditional love.

The symbol in the barley had become a fixation in the brotherhood. Someone in the Crow's Nest had commented that it was "the last straw." Others laughingly agreed that it was the end. He was now to be considered totally unreliable, worse than useless, dangerous, unless . . .

Truly the time had come as Baphomet had prophesied: the myth would one day be made real. The people had had enough. They demanded the real thing now, the sacrifice of the one who kept getting away with everything, eluding them, driving them all crazy, until "the world can't tell right from wrong!" someone said.

The Temple would put a stop to it. Judgment Day, the New World Order was here at last. They had the technology to pull it off, with or without him. The messianic middle man could be sacrificed, at last. The people would be relieved. The kingdom was at hand, arising from the deep.

Meanwhile, the Indian love had made two unspoken statements that danced before his eyes: "I am an American woman! And you are the Running Christ."

If the first truth sounded out of touch, coming from a people that he automatically relegated to the past, the second truth pressed him like an outrageous tax claim or the voice of a creditor with ludicrous demands and unwarranted powers.

Yes, he was obviously the Christ! It fit and it felt as close as his own skin. He devoured the truth of it so fast that he was instantaneously convinced that he already knew. So many signs had pointed that way. Of course he had always known! Only modesty and manners had held him back from confirming it to himself. But that was no problem now, because everyone knew that Jesús was incredibly modest. He went for the credits like a gambler cashing in, on the defensive.

He had to be quick about it, because she would as quickly take them away, and more.

He was checking his balance, his image.

As for those tales, he looked into the screen and chanted in his mind with the firestorms that spoke for him, saving him from exposure, allowing him a few moments of reflection, silencing him, eating away at him, because he was powerless to drop the mask and harangue her.

He owed them for the mask and the armor! The entire panoply was his— His thing! On credit, and nothing more.

The power of the people would undo him, as surely as the Indian woman nearby. He was so close to them all, scrambling for his crown, while they kept handing it to him, adjusting it on his head, dusting him off, while she told tales of the running man, or Christ.

Many of them had driven themselves to commit atrocities to enforce a claim that simply was not true. In past lives, he had managed to maintain a leadership role, enough to give their wild assertions a grain of truth, enough to keep many of them sane, keep them from having to enforce the claim to ridiculous and diabolical extremes everyday of their lives. Untold millions had been held hostage and sacrificed to his success in life and in protection from the guilt.

But these days, in Central Maine, he was really in danger of being just another guy, trying to connect it all up on the old Benedict Arnold Trail. He was so far out of program that they were asserting madcap images of him in frenzies whipped up in the new technology to levels never before seen in the history of his religion, the sort of thing that explodes into the hundreds and thousands of tin gods and heroes. Orpheus! Christ! Christ consciousness! The Orphic Force!

Out of the Chronicles paraded the hokey little doodad Westerns, cornball sitcoms, heroic serial killers in the shinning armor of the big screen. He was going the way the West was lost.

The Serapis had snowballed so far out of control that God was devouring him, an empty cliché in search of a word for itself, for the word made flesh: Him. And he'd kept reincarnating into more and more flesh and blood. It was a scientific fact. The hallelujahs were falling flat, the country and Western music wheezed and whined in the new technology.

Equality, responsibility, immortality of the soul that returns in different races, different social circumstances, different environments that it has left behind—he had discussed it with such programmed eloquence, but he knew it in his soul, and it was polarizing him in the wheel. They raged in his ears, "Don't look back!"

He had run to nature, back to the temple dance, where he could experience the love of the gods and collect at the watering hole. Now there was the Indian female. And the addicted multitude, the "addicti," as he had often referred to them in science: they were calling for the sacrifice. "Don't look back!" translated into: "Sacrifice it!"

He knew about that tension.

If he flinched now. If he looked like he would take off the creditworthy mask of the "good fellow," they seethed with anxiety: "Do nothing! We'll do it for you! Don't look back! Look how angry we are, we're enraged! See? See the rage? Don't look back! You'd better not look back because, if you do— Just don't look back, see? Do not try it! Don't look . . . back . . ." The threats seethed with tormented memories, long personal histories of hell on earth.

If he looked like he would keep the faith, they were in raptures, victorious: "Don't look back! Don't look back! Don't look back!—onwards and upwards!" Either way, the words said it all. They were out of control, out of their minds, "Don't look back."

He blamed it on the Indian woman, listened to the frenzied madness and rage in the speakers, felt the sounds take hold of him with a renewed hunger. He froze in the loop between the Temple and the temple dance.

Every slightest ragged edge of rage that he might call his own—that tore away from his emotions held in trust by the temple, muffled and distant (all so strategically given expression at key times by the immense powers of the cybercult)—that raged in his eyes and flickered in her direction backed up on him when the imprisoning sound that emerged from that technology compensated with an extra burst of sound and light, reminding him, exhorting him, dividing him from himself with the words implicit everywhere he looked—Don't look back! And all he wanted was to join in the chant, into the luxury of rage.

He couldn't think. The little rags of angry poverty made him envious of the motherlode out there, behind the screen.

From within the world's most luxuriant panoply of armor, he began to loathe and fear his poverty of feeling, as though he were about to be tortured by the iron maidens: Christian virgins in Christian dungeons filled with the sacrificial knives reserved for heretics like him, if he steps out of line, and they close the door, whoever . . . anyone, anonymous, out of control, Some One in the name of One Something.

His hate escalated. It felt like a benediction. He was one of them, one of the people, to some extent. He had a role to play. It now seemed clear. But it was a freezing mask. It began to look into nothing, going nowhere. He demanded the heat, the fires in the hateful sound.

He expected it to melt him, but instead it had claws that were squeezing him with the pressures of the emotions in the noise. He felt the cold blood drip from the wounds. He saw himself as the eye in the cybercult. He realized that those addicti felt like him. They vented their rage against nature. They were a society in long-term shock, collapsing, being sacrificed by themselves, self-destructing. He realized why he was so characterless in the slipstream system. He rediscovered himself now as their messiah.

Fiery lights danced in rings against the dark screen. The

randomizing assertions crediting anything and everything in the cult, all the programs at once in a frenzied mutual admiration of panoplies designed to attack with the words, "don't look back," suddenly fused into the very sounds of the words themselves, in English: "Don't look back." They dissolved, then resolved themselves like the eye of the people trying to focus on him, stare him down with their credits: "Don't look back!" It threatened, commanded and prayed, as he stared back, back into the monitor.

It was textured and mixed by the babble of languages assembled in the system, calling on him directly: "Don't look back." The virtual dials at Glass Farm and the Crow's Nest were carefully adjusted up and down.

Now was his cue. It was time for him to move outside, to take center stage, to attempt his return to the Temple, complete the cycle. He was with them. He would save them and somehow save himself.

He had collected love, the deep golden mystery of absolute wealth. Now he must bring the credits home to the brotherhood, the family. He could feel them rejoice with anticipation. There would be a great sacrifice. A millennial, a multi-millennial climax, and all the tension would be relieved. The beast would grow fatter than a thousand suns. Everything could be controlled.

He got up stiffly and walked out of the room.

"There he goes," said Sam. "Run, run—" she stopped herself with a worried look.

D—Dagaz, day, dawn, rebirth of the light, fulfillment.

# 16. Under Starlight

THE FOUR LOVERS IN GLASTONBURY HAD been watching the harvesters at work. The backdoor data crystal was polarized and clear. They had watched the subtlest changes in Jesús's expression.

It had not occurred to them that the Temple were not only delighted to have the lovers there, "backstage" with the gods, they were illuminated, enraptured. Project Light Center was in backroom bliss.

The programmed trivialization of these backdoor servants, players, gods and hangers-on contradicted the fact that the entire programmed cybercult depended on the low status and priority of nature's life force, the slipstream, the pathways of the love of the gods.

The ever-so-Puckish back room was making a clumsy little show of being comfortably ensconced backstage, good-fellows one and all, with the rest of the common folk, gods, heroes and everyone up on screen, up in the Crow's Nest, raptured away like glistening plastics on a shelf disappearing into cyberspace, swept into a vanishing point. They interacted with the Glass Farm Craft Center.

The lovers played their parts animal-like, instinctively, visibly in the dark, guided by the intermittent lights over invisible streams of logic. Nature's love seemed so vast in its intimacy and limitless communication that the idea of this love being lower down in someone's personal hierarchy was ludicrous, difficult to grasp for very long and uncomfortable to hold.

But the serpent was lost in the maze. Though the idea that the little backdoor art-box might be "clear" served up delights previously unimagined by the screen-watchers on the main system's widespread integrated data crystal, they wanted to be sure that the situation didn't get "out of hand," as Lancelot had advised, what with the latest crop circle and the Shakespeare monument. It was quaint, to be sure, but the backdoor art-box was supposed to be a system driver. It must not become the mainstream, or the show was obviously in trouble. They would not be fooled by Puck, whoever he may be. Minimize him but not too much!

"Of course, he is more than just a rabbit!" one monk indignantly explained. It was incomprehensible that anyone with real power would go about like that, with those big ears and all, the bunny rabbit tail. What ego could deal with such a thing as a cosmically powerful force behaving in this way?

The whole fairy troupe could only be taken seriously as a necessary part of the planetary system, no more. Just one of the life forms found on the earth, just like the others, found elsewhere, most everywhere!—

It was the craft of a helmsman to make the gods a proper part of the wheel. If nature was not chasing the mainstream, then the wheel would collapse. Millions of willing hostages in carefully tailored panoply was the craft. Nature spirits cared. They would try to free the people. That was the juice for the spin that usurped the slipstream.

Like any technology, this wheel had to be maintained, if the brothers wanted to escape the Running Christ, filled with tales and gossip, where the One Omniscient Circle of God lapses into mythology. Wheels within wheels haunted them always and pushed their exuberance to extremes.

Just to be certain, to craft the right balance of pressures on the helm, Lancelot himself was advised to go out to the recently formed crop circle and do a small dance, a balancing act that would ensure a safety net. He was allowed to bring along some of the accepted worshippers of Isis, Gaia or Cybele, if he, himself, on consultation with the dialed-up channels, found the energy to be exact.

☙ ❧

The lovers by the Tor saw Jesús leave the farmhouse. The front door slammed as though the place were of little account. He strutted into the night like an actor approaching center stage. A blinding white spotlight pinned him in mid stride.

It caught him in a secret moment of his own, dislodging him from the surroundings. It held him in the intimate presence of his past lives, where the suppressed routines that were running crazy in three words—"Don't look back!"—were now unwinding his own soap operas, in the spotlight.

He began to mutter incoherently the repetitive denials programmed to service his mask, his visor, the armor, the expensive wardrobe. The repetitions of unformed words wheeled in his mind, like a roulette wheel that never stops, always on edge with the promise of the big win. The tension was beyond endurance. He lacked the energy to free up the wheel, bring back the game.

He thought of Sam. He was suddenly convinced that she had something that belonged to him, that was rightfully his, like a piece of his costume. He would go back and get it.

"Don't look back!" came the chant out of the night sky.

He froze, his knees gave way, he staggered with stage fright. He didn't have it to give.

It would have been just an act, a ritual performance. The sacrifice of his blood and body would have been just a few credits, tokens of panoply for everyone who had made a contribution to the cybercult. A small cycle of energy representing the whole wheel of insurance. An inspiration and a forgiveness. A salutary reminder that one needn't necessarily look back all that often. It wasn't really blood and flesh, even if they said it was . . . it wasn't really. The old wagon wheel was sinking into the rut.

He fell to his knees, babbling and chattering in terror. The ritual was becoming real. The gamble was no longer affordable: the addiction was eating him alive. It was the program of cannibalism, of his actually being eaten. He felt the reality of it catch up with him, like teeth into his own flesh, lips sucking his own blood. He began to scream.

The choirs of chaos burst into angelic harmonies inside his head: "Don't look back, don't look back!" overlaid with the lyrics, "Blood and body, blood and body!"

The mask was gone, the armor was shredding away, the addicti were berserk in their hopeless insistence, hungering, devouring, every credit turning into a debt cannibalizing him, unpackaging him for the feast, about to devour themselves if they didn't get him. The great routine balancing act was over.

The Temple were applauding and shaking hands. It was all according to plan. This was better than the original plan, as foretold.

He had chosen not to believe within the system. This was the ultimate sacrifice. The old religion would pass and the new image of God would begin. The old God would be reborn.

The tension of living blindly with the reality of a reincarnating ordinary-sort-of-a guy-type Christ was driving the West off the rails and taking the world with it. Democracy was reaching out. He had to be eaten now, once and for all.

Of course, something had to arrive in his place. A piece of it now shined its light upon him from above.

He screamed and screamed.

Then he stopped.

He began to proclaim himself. He would not go without an attempt to regain control of that beast in shinning armor.

Samantha and John were outside in a heartbeat, while Bellarose had run upstairs to check on the children.

A spotlight each hit them as they came out the door. The lights darted this way and that, looking for a hook. John's trained military reflexes took over. With an arm around Sam, they crouched down and zigzagged a few paces. She got the message, and they confused the enemy long enough to reach the shelter of some trees. They were scared; plenty of panoply to lift them both into the light, no doubt—whatever this Jesus may have thought.

But the two spotlights were withdrawn and replaced with shadows that angled in and out among those of branches under the usurping moon-beast.

Sam and John quietly circled round the garden and approached Jesús, but he called out: "Get back! No, stay away from me!" He wouldn't look at them, but held out his hand against them.

They found that it presented a wall of energy, and they could not advance any further. They pressed against it.

He looked up at the beast and laughed, "I am in my box! My box, not yours! You have your own box, this is mine, my box! You go away!" And he began to babble unintelligibly, as though speaking in tongues.

He was Ptolemy, the mad Pharaoh and god. He was not afraid to die in battle! What truth to the rumors? Nothing to die for? He had plenty to die for! Plenty! Who would say he did not have plenty? "Pharaoh has plenty! Egypt never starves! Egypt feeds the world! Egypt will feed Rome! Egypt will feed the Greeks! Everyone will eat! And they will know the wealth of the Nile, and they will credit it! Serapis will be theirs! The One God with the cap of grain on his head! And the wolf-dog by his side! They will eat it! Eat him, yes . . . eat him . . . Pharaoh gives plenty and is not afraid to die! It is not true that the people are starving! Lies! Lies! They eat me with their lies! Ptolemy was never a coward in battle with Alexander! Alexander was a madman! A drunk. Running, running after the women, the women of Bacchus! Drunken democracy, debauchery . . . He would do anything at all! Just lucky! Lucky Ptolemy lives! Lives to be eaten!—

"To be eaten?" The reality attacked full force. He clutched his skin over and over. He rolled round on the ground, groaning. He turned inadvertently towards the doorway where Bellarose had appeared, joined by the other two in retreat. "Help!" he yelled. "Help, ye gods! Help! Help me! Help!" He howled it, "Heeeellllp," long and hard, like a wolf. Then he gave a long wolf call, as though it would never stop. It cycled up and down, howl upon howl, ending with little gasps of breath, "Help, help, help!" almost muttering to himself as an afterthought. Then the howls started up again.

One of the gods spoke back, conjured through Bellarose: "Oooooo! Bubble bubble, toil and nothin' but trouble!" It was JB, the bear.

Jesús continued to howl up and down.

Then the cockney voice of PC came to the scene, " 'Ello, 'ello, 'ello! Wot's this, then? Wot 'ave we 'ere!"

Jesús went quiet. Sam and John were scrutinizing Bellarose.

The beast backed off, the spotlight went out.

John looked up at the black shadow that blocked out the stars. "It's still there."

PC, courtesy of Bellarose, amazed at herself, like an actor improvising with nature's inspiration, picked up a smooth beaver-chewed stick that they kept by the door and swung it like a policeman's baton. "Best get 'im inside; 'owlin' at the moon on a moonless night! I ask you! Can't 'ave that, now! 'Tain't natural-like, disturbin' the peace, if you know wot I mean!"

Sam and John went and got him up off the grass. But he wouldn't come inside.

☙ ❧

Tanya, Julie, Jack and Lawrence were watching as the slipstream camera carried their empathetic, wordless attention from one scene to the next. A pooka had just stepped out from behind a tree by the farmhouse, turned itself into an English bobby and walked to merge with Bellarose, who had appeared briefly as herself, when a polar bear had turned back into a white light and flown like a meteor into the Big Dipper.

As the gods spoke, they appeared on screen in her place, while she became invisible, to reappear whenever she had something to say. The lovers watched and realized that they too were in the troupe of the overlapping trails of souls in lights, in on the act, open to channel some inspiration, knowingly or not. The slipstream camera returned to closed curtains on stage. Instrumental music played and improvised, as though for an intermission.

Jack finally said, "Well . . ." and trailed off.

Tanya turned down the sound.

"Well wot? If you know wot I mean." Lawrence grinned, which provoked a shove from Julie.

"Well well well," Jack continued. "That poor fuck!— Easy to say. I might have saved him the trouble. Coulda woulda shoulda. Still—a quick and timely installation of the crop circle." He sighed. "Back when I was a screen-watcher."

"They woulda been on you like a cat on a rat," Tanya consoled.

"They slammed me anyway."

"Excuse me," said Julie, "but just how would that 'installation'—whatever that means—have helped?"

"The crop circle," he replied with slow sadness, "was formed as a true symbol of just who my old buddy Jesús is. Truth of his character is woven into the language of the circle, with the help of Bellarose and John."

Tanya picked up the pace, "When merged with the Shakespeare monument, it cleared our data crystal in the art-box here, spectacularly! The runes told the larger truth, including what we had figured out together."

"Yeah, ya gotta have backup. We got your back, Jack!" said Julie, and threw her arms around him.

They saw his eyes well up as he smiled, and added, "Well, we all ran back here, didn't we, lovers?" He quietly gave way to the tears.

"Sad init!" said Lawrence ironically, his eyes shinning. Then he succumbed to a group hug, once Tanya had folded in.

Recovering, Jack confessed, "I just wasn't being true to myself, just another Running Christ trying to be something I wasn't, a screen-ogling idiot, a bit of artificial, phoney intelligence, a programmed algorithm for a wheel going nowhere, judgmental, pretending to be balanced, especially with us four. I am so . . . so sorry. Broke us up."

The group hug broke up, as they sat up and listened.

"Anyone who claims perfection claims chaos," he continued with the aphorism. "Perfect symmetries of repetition require random chaos, the supposedly exactly repeating units of the roulette wheel? It's a major problem in our math and software languages. Can't get it outa the coding. I shoulda known that, anyway. There I go again." He trailed off.

"But," he doubled down, "had the system known the basic, asymmetric truth, it would have balanced out in a renewed sense of polarity, with a real sense of direction, with love, not just what sex you are! It would have stopped the dependency, the feeding frenzy!—

"I was just a scrap, food for the paradox, keep it lookin' good."

"The polarity of no absolute poles?" said Julie suggestively, to lighten him up. "Finger lickin' good?"

"It unconsciously assumes its own destruction in the End of All Things—Armageddon! when everything is devastated, eaten up. It cries out for the fake mythological Judgment Day and sacrifice. Fake because it can never happen absolutely—spoiler alert!

"It's a typical monofier. It depends on an absolute God of some sort, a croupier to put the brake on. The divine neutrality is supposed to control the monofiers gone randomly mad.

"There's no such thing, of course. Pure neutrality is again just another case of that symmetrical randomness. So nature's powerfully nuanced polarity, without the help of any one absolute god, reveals the running man."

"*Mansplaining* again, honey?" Tanya couldn't resist slowing him up, after Julie's attempt.

"No straight lines in nature," he persisted, "no perfectly closed circles, either," he ruminated. "So it's not a true wheel, it's a fake—like me."

"Well, he sure runs himself down, all right!" said Lawrence. "Love exists. His own soul stops his program, when he's with nature, eventually. It's love's polarity in nature's plenty, the symbol in the grain, if I might say so. Where's that fresh loaf we bought?"

"The word made flesh?" suggested Tanya.

"Neveh mind."

"Well, quick!" said Julie. "All we gotta do is get the main system to access the crop circle!"

"The Temple's blocking it with their Running Christ," said Lawrence, "as long as 'he's out there all messed up. It just hasn't put it together. That's their gamble, their crafted, artsy gamble."

"What if we go out and open up the slipstream, somehow?" asked Tanya. "Find a way to make the connection?"

"Where? Anywhere? Randomly?" said Julie.

"It's already onto us, all right," said Lawrence. "P'raps it would care to follow us there, where that circle is."

"It's more than just a circle," said Julie.

"I know that!"

The slipstream camera took them there on screen, without further ado. They watched a Cybelian orgy in progress in the middle of the symbol in the field by the Craft Center, Lancelot Camelot holding the knife to his genitals, for ritual display.

Small exuberant remarks circulated in the castle tower.

"Now what!" said Jack bitterly. "Where are we now? They've got this thing sewed up. They're selectively blocking us, monitoring every detail, taking special care not to get too close or too far."

"Sharpish!" said Lawrence.

"What if their end of the system just had a peek into our screen, for example?" said Julie. "It'd see what the gods wanted it to see. It's in their hands, the camera: all clear! Then it would catch on and the main data crystal would clear itself up the rest of the way."

"So what does that say?" said Tanya. "It's in the lap of the gods. Or more likely, the message is to stay where we are and follow the camera ourselves, don't freak out! Don't despair!"

"What wit' everyone off their 'eads and the like!"

"Lance angling for promotion to the Vatican choir as one of the castrati," she added.

"Take them back to their roots," said Julie. "After all, it was Cybele's Vatican Hill—and her eunuchs were priests, same as today or perhaps tomorrow . . . who knows, any moment now . . . they could all get the rapture and history comes to life in one slip o' the knife."

The atmosphere in the room let up somewhat. They saw the level of programmed ritual frenzy at the crop circle tighten up correspondingly and lose track of itself, its controlled exuberance. The dancers were stumbling into themselves and the camera left them there, Lancelot still intact.

It presented the lovers with a view of the earth from space.

Arteries of light poured down like rainbows becoming waterfalls, focused into specific sites in the ground. The slipstream camera zoomed down the rainbow falls, revealing patterns like the bark of a magic tree, with roots that could be seen to feed the world. The branches disappeared into the starlit heavens, warm with familiar places to travel, reminding them of what the earth could become, had been, still is, wherever those branches of the world trees are felt in the land, in the soul.

The planetary organism glowed with the gift of life. They could see the fever that burned the ocean between the coasts of Africa and America. The infection was being drawn out along the drowning shores of Europe and North America and from the melting poles, out of Antarctica, down from Northern waters.

Instead of an ocean, there was a fire with usurping roots of infection tugging at the land. The flames were white where a piece of technology left over from ancient days, a spherical world within a wheel rising from within the slipstream world of the ocean, was being lifted into the social human world by the continuous blocking and withholding of the slipstream's power as they chanted, "Don't look back," holding open the door between worlds, hanging onto the past in desperation and ignorance, in the wheel of the cult.

The lovers were taken aback. Not because the ship was so alien but because it was so familiar, all of a sudden, a memory. They recognized it, and that fact shocked them into the wider reality.

"So," said Tanya, "it's like we've been living in the Middle Ages, going along with this phony little pretense that the world is flat and that we are the center of the cosmos, just playing along with the conventions, when all along, of course, this is the way it is, obviously! So . . . it's the suburbs . . . of the galaxy . . . all this history and warfare goin' on, and our thing has been to just pretend otherwise, like it's not happening here. We're not supposed to admit it. I admit it, I'm a fool, that's all!"

"Oi, easy!" said Lawrence. "This thing's bound t' have an effect, not to put too fine a point on it. So . . . it's all right, know wot I mean?"

They could hear the chanting, "Don't look back, don't look back," in a single roar, as though the people were erupting with the threshold.

"I almost wish I didn't know what they were saying," said Julie. "Whoever's got that camera or whoever's in charge of the sound . . . I wish they'd turn it down—or off!"

"The knob's right there, obvious—" commented Jack under his breath, trying not to be sarcastic.

"What?"

"Nothing . . . sorry. I was just remembering . . . what a certain mural . . . and the words . . . The body of our Lord, Jesus Christ . . . I don't think I'm panicking. I'm just talking along here, that's all. If I say something weird, forget it."

"What's that noise?" said Julie.

"Sounds like wolves," said Tanya.

It grew louder as the audiences responded to their Leader of the Ages. They had followed him for forgotten reasons, established in worlds of hierarchies based on age and descent, taken for granted until his leadership was but a reflex among the people. They just reacted in program, depending on their relationship to the cult. He had dropped everything and howled. They were dropping, "Don't look back!"

He was joining them, they were joining him; together they were howling like a pack of wolves. He was still their leader, regardless of whichever church or temple he now proclaimed, as ever.

They went along with the Master of the Wheel, howling at nothing, going nowhere, just howling and howling with the Leader of the Pack.

The camera returned to him, out in the garden, under the stars.

U—Uruz, male energy, the aurochs, an extinct buffalo.

# 17. The Green Man

SAM AND JOHN WERE CALLED BACK into the farmhouse by PC. They had to leave Jesús there; he would not come. They had waited by him, and he had begun to howl once more. He had kept it up, and they had wondered what to do. Now they waited with the lovers, for the gods to inspire the next move.

Sam went to turn off the screen but quickly returned with a look on her face of shock and amusement. "They're howling on TV, too, the whole damn world, it seems, like a pack o' wolves or coyotes . . . so is the anchor man . . . and that Barbara woman. They're howling in there. On TV."

She leaned against the soft liquid lights that seemed to stream along the varnished wooden walls and took in the breeze of a nearby fan. "And they've killed off almost every wolf in the world. Always open season on ol' Coyote. And now they want to take his place. Stand up for something, ha! Christians and sheep. Some flock!"

She refused to succumb to any bitterness, the shock or even the humor, and cooled herself out some more, listening to the howling man in the garden at the end of his bi-millennial run.

Titania looked at them through Bellarose's eyes and spoke in sultry southern inflections, "Haven't we had enough of this? If they were real-life wolves howlin' at the moon, that would be one thing. But it's a new blue moon tonight."

She swayed gently and straightened her back, rocked her hips a little and turned to Sam with a smile. "What do you think? Is there a moon like that, honey?"

"He should be made to run round in circles—singing the gingerbread song."

"Why don't you go ask him?"

"OK, I will!"

Samantha gracefully stepped out the door. She approached Jesús with Indian care. She noticed that the shadow in the sky was still present. He was looking up at it. She put her hand against his chest and felt the vibration of his voice. She realized that he was asserting himself at least partly in order to keep the shadow away. She listened to be sure.

He allowed her to soothe him with her hand round his side and to the back where she massaged him and pressed her fingers against the solar plexus from the back. She pressed some pressure points of shiatsu. She lit some sage.

His noise subsided enough for him to hear her whisper in his ear, "Together we can make it go away!"

The smoke wafted. He stopped howling and looked at her in the dark, with light from the windows.

"Say it," she whispered. "Say, 'Run . . . run . . . run . . .' " She blushed, and he felt the warmth of it in the change of atmosphere.

"Go on." She put one hand out and took hold of his. "Say, 'Run, run . . . just as fast as you can . . .' "

The spotlight reached for them both.

She held his hand and said firmly, "Let's go! In a circle!" She danced around him, slowly at first, keeping hold of his hand, turning him round, the strong scented coils interfering with the glare from above. "Sing! Run, run, run . . . Sing it loud! Run run run!" Her voice caressed him like big calm chords that rose and fell.

"Now! Run run run, round this big oak tree!— See?"

The spotlight was slipping this way and that, looking for the hooks of addiction.

In one quick motion, she cast the sage into and aromatic arc and pulled off her T-shirt. She wiped hot sweat from her brow.

His face lit up. She lifted off the loose bra she wore when she was around him, because he would so often make her feel uncomfortable. She felt freer, fighting back, protesting with her sex.

He lit up some more, and they went round the tree singing together the Gingerbread Man song, like they should be locked up.

The shadow vanished.

The slipstream continued to open up.

The shock waves reverberated into the darkness of the pupil of the eye on screen, where the dancing lights, supposed to be transmitted as special effects by the Crow's Nest, scattered as a series of disturbances across the screens of the audiences.

Some kept up the howling, while others began to laugh, hearing the howling howl back at them from the system with the occasional screech of feedback.

The scene with the beach and the ocean reappeared on all screens with the ship visible half above the waves, under the sunny stars of the brightly lit stage. The nameplate with *Eurydice* in typewriter font came into view.

The slipstream players looked upon it with dismay. This was supposed to be their performance, not some usurping ET ship naming itself after a tree spirit, no longer able to withstand the anonymity of the Underworld, presumably. They were not unaccustomed to outlandish events, being so somewhat themselves. But this! Seriously!

From offstage, round the corner of the fantastic trees and beyond the curtains, the world audience distinctly heard a voice say: "It's a hoax."

"Yeah, that's it," said another, "a hoax! With the U.N.? Holy cow!"

The idea spread along the slipstream, until so many had repeated it in homes, arenas, online that one of the anchors finally had to take the microphone away from the howlers and report flatly that reports are coming in from sources that say it's a hoax, fake news.

At that moment everything turned ugly and dangerous.

Groups of the addicti began to call for the sacrifice of the blood and body. They were sure they had been promised.

But he was getting hot running round the old oak tree singing with the Indian woman, "Run run run just as fast as you can, can't catch me, I'm the Gingerbread Man!" Over and over until they fell to the grass in each other's arms, sheltered from the world view. The lovers by the Tor saw the storied face of the Green Man emerge in the oaken wood with an ivy-laced smile.

Bellarose and John stood in the doorway, arms round each other's waist, looking back with the love of the greenwood embracing them. There were fairy lights and torchlight on wands afoot in the extensive gardens and nearby woods and the brook. There was song, adapted from the Bard's *As You like It*.

Under the greenwood tree,
Who loves to lie with me,
And turn a merry note
Unto the sweet bird's throat,

Come hither, come hither, come hither:
Here shall we see
No enemy
But winter and rough weather.

Who doth ambition shun,
And loves to live in the sun,
Seeking the food we eat,
And pleased with what we get,
Come hither, come hither, come hither:
Here shall we see
No enemy
But winter and rough weather.

ଓ ଃ

While Sam and Jesús were quietly divesting themselves of pretense amid the sylvan enchantment, the Gingerbread Man chant took hold in the wide world. The extra-flat-spoken anchor who had seized the higher reality was giving out that further sources were reporting chants of "Run run run, just as fast as you can, can't catch me, I'm the Gingerbread Man."

Things were getting uglier and uglier in many quarters. No sacrifice in sight to resolve the extraterrestrial-type expectation that was to resolve the tension of the programmed randomizing "Don't look back"—gingerbread men and women on the run with threats and promises of status and power, advancement, lifetime to lifetime, in the cybercult. The Crow's Nest were beginning to wonder if they were in trouble.

A lot of people who had tuned in to stay informed were now raiding the refrigerator or making their way to get hotdogs, soft drinks and popcorn, getting a little horny all the while. Some were thinking of getting home before something went totally wrong with the crowds.

In the absence of a sacrifice to break the random tension of a wheel that was designed to usurp the sun and moon, a devouring chain reaction that was supposed to generate the energy of order in society, this absence of sacrifice randomly began to devour the addicti wherever it found them—technology in the sacred hands, sacrificial knives. Here and there the screaming erupted. Flesh was torn from bone by strangers, by family, by self, teeth breaking on bone.

The people were not required to be the ultimate saviors, though they had been recruited for the sacrifice, many of them in past lives. So they generally were inclined to transfer that role onto the handiest savior they could find, anyone looking innocent enough, enjoying themselves with hotdog, adding plenty of mustard and ketchup, relish, when they should be showing some respect!

It was about to be a long night for any of the police still on duty. "Crowd control" was a small description for what was to be required of them, if the event fell into abject chaos. The new anchor man with the heightened sense of reality was appealing for calm. He soon lost the microphone to another, then another, as they peeled off and joined song and dance of death.

All the screens were depicting the blank shadowy silver and white of the Great Kingdom from within the mysterious depths, the oceanic underworld, where it had lodged itself to suck the blood of the planet. It was hanging and floating at sea level, half way through the threshold between the world of its ancient flyways and the tangible planetary fields of energy we call Earth.

There was a kerfuffle in the Crow's Nest. The languid sarcasm had become foreshortened into acerbic commands and cynical acknowledgments. The all-too-pleased courtesies were losing their understated fervor, as they struggled to make a programmed transition to the philosophical frown. The power-playing zeal was being set aside.

The boys at the top were not the engineers or inventors. Typically, they were investors, private equity people, well removed and ensconced in their armor of credits and debits. They were now among the most vulnerable to the ripping away. In their long history of crisis management and asset stripping, the program had been to revert to a previous program and sell out to some sucker. All they knew was that they could not afford to listen to any "bright ideas" from some of the more "creative" brothers lower down, if they wished to remain on top when everything was at stake.

In their experience, the only familiar thing about this crisis was that they were in danger of losing their positions, so they froze up and reverted to program. An impressive credibility ritual was in order.

Those remaining at the Crows Nest and Glass Farm decided to fake the climax of the sacrifice with electronic blood and body. Their most creditworthy news anchors would stand by the altar, as priests, to give the ultimate "factual report." In times of crisis, no one could fill the "pulpit of truth" like a reporter, as any three-headed media gatekeeper knows. What would Cerberus do?

The sacrifice would be based on science and society. And the great sea monster was poking its head into the world. That would help. After all, it was a powerhouse of programs. If it would just take over at some point, get a good hook and reel itself in, all would be well.

It was a gamble, but their antisocial programs had been so long in power, they suddenly felt lucky and were up for a good swash-buckle. The software brothers chattered into the system's microphones and tapped at keyboards.

A deep voice came to the ears of the world. "O people! Ye have been tested. I, Serapis, God of Gods, who am called by the names of the faithful, God of All Things, Maker of Heaven and Earth, I speak!"

He got their attention. The hotdogs were blocked on the way to the mouths. Wolf-pack humans ceased their howls, and their hangers-on decided to give up pretending. No one felt particularly horny anymore. The screams were systematically tuned out, muffled by the bespoke panoplies. This voice was the sound of the moral imperative. They all recognized it, most respected it, hated it, were silenced by it. They knew the old God when they heard him, and he still had the stuff to shut them up for a short while. Every word counted, none to be wasted now. "Bring on the sacrifice!"

A typical flying saucer zigzagged down to the top of the alien sea monster. It was the little beast, back from Archon, empty and hungry, returned without the Christ. It emitted devouring vibes.

A door opened, and a gangplank was lowered from its belly. The doorway exuded a cloud of white smoke that tightened and turned red. Claws reappeared, and the eye opened.

Angel wings unfolded on either side of the eye. It flapped and alighted down the gangplank. Two bare legs and angelically translucent feet in sandals extended from a loincloth and torso. The eye closed, turning the lid into a face, while the smoke became a halo filtering a piercing light from back inside the oval saucer of obsolete technology, in nature's theater.

The face was the mask of Jesús de l'Orient. The empty cybertype walked down the plank and down the side of the ship that now receded in the photography, bringing into the foreground again the beach where the enhanced crashing of the waves was brought gently to the ears of the audience.

He stepped down onto the water and continued towards the beach. There was a close-up of his expression, impassive, friendly, accepting, as Jesús would have done it. A donkey ride into Jerusalem could not have expressed it better.

It was the typical program: the young Aztec, filled with the purpose of the cult, as he approached the bloodstained steps of the pyramid, to begin his ascent to heaven, to the sun god, the Devouring One, who would honor him in the memory of the people, as a member of the Divine Family, one of the devouring multitude, forever, lost in time, without great significance, until one Day of Judgment, when the Master himself, the Helmsman, Captain and Architect, will, for the first and last time, live in his own House of God, after all others who have been chosen for the sacrifice have gone before him, with an eye for an eye, a tooth for a tooth, a ship going down for a ship resurrected in chaos, according to ritual.

His day had finally come, when the ritual in name alone, building tension, was coming to an end, after being worn down without release, by all those who had been sacrificed in the ways of war, the peaceful ways, religious ways, legal ways, political and economic ways, with pomp and ceremony or cast aside, dragon slayers in natural poses to be recorded for future playback in the armor of this and that type. It was now coming to an end, at last.

This was the New World Order. The true Jesus, sacrificed for real, no escape, no twin, no run to the Americas to start over again in the New World.

He stepped onto the sandy beach and was met by the man with the microphone who invited him to the front of the stage, to come to the altar for a brief interview, after which he would lie down on the marble slab and await the knife. He would keep the mask all the way, the system would see to it. No screaming.

With every step he took, the audience became more and more respectful, amazed and aghast. But many of them hurried to finish the hotdogs and soft drinks in a kind of frenzy of survival, like it might be their last, and they might be out of place. Many hurried to conform, on their knees. But there were a lot of folk who recognized a good tale when they saw one. Or so say I! They were into it, after so many cheap chronicles.

They noticed things happening in the background. There were eruptions in the monster's strangely metallic skin, and the ocean was changing color, while the waves began to crash for real, in ways that were somehow unreal to the sacrifice, or more than real, with an awakening power.

The brief, preliminary talk show was stalled. The image of Jesús was strangely oblivious to the rising storm and the surf that was threatening the sacrifice. His back seemed resolutely to the weather.

In the Crow's Nest, the brothers were working in a silent fever at the system's keys and metaphors. They were losing it. Not enough people were buying it. Too many were enjoying it in the wrong way. The theatrical spirit of the ceremony was being appreciated as the audiences began to work to discover the point of view of the script. Why was he just standing there like that?

Weren't they going to rip out his heart or something?

Crucify him?

There's no cross, and he's not responding to the anchorman.

There's no sound for the voices.

Have they lost the sound or just forgotten their lines?

Is this live?

You just can't trust the media these days!

Always acting like know-it-alls and socialites!

Talkin' down to people all the time!

They just don't believe in anything but themselves, and not even that!

Certainly don't believe in equality.

They're supposed to believe in democracy!

What's to believe? Like it's some religion?

Everybody's got an angle!

Pretendin' they're neutral, cynical bastards!

Ideas like these were circulating on the slipstream, calling on a media that was crying out as though it had been boxed in by freedom, crying wolf, selling freedom, selling free speech, freedom in a box, going nowhere, saying nothing, howling, Oooyyyez! Ooooyyyez! You've been cheated! Freedom's collapsing on you! Look at us, falling apart, looking at you! Oyez! Oooooyeah! Ahwooooo!

The main data crystal was integrating its memory with the symbol in the grain, logging onto the art-box, remembering, while the demons of the Underworld writhed in their own threshold between worlds, forgetting everything in shock, the slipstream backing up on them as the blocking mythologies gave way to the humor, the insight of a growing margin of the audience, a wave generating more waves of recognition.

The image of Christ vanished and reappeared several times, finally to be withdrawn from the scene. The anchorman backed out. The stone altar disappeared, and the camera panned the horizon to reveal the storm filled with wheels of lights, sheet lightning and thunderbolts.

The slipstream was opening up as seldom seen in history. The extraterrestrial invader was being eaten by its own threshold. The communicating door closed on it definitively, squeezing its juices to the wind. The slipstream carried the shock waves of the collapsing threshold into the weather systems of the planet, into the consciousness that runs through the geological structures of the earth, integrating the pressures, according to the tension in the people, according to the polarity of their personal slipstreams. Their combined past actions generated, cancelled and amplified the vast slipstream waves, moment by moment, resonating the maze of history. The gods translated the tensions into temperature differences, building into extreme highs and lows that cycled a tropical depression increasingly into a hurricane, organizing, absorbing and containing the attack on the planet, wheeling the foe with t'ai chi, integrating the evil energy all the more, exhausting it, recycling it.

The lovers recognized the lights in the storm. They instinctively felt the deep emotion in the weather. Julie had spoken of this poetry in the climate, how it could be extended along the slipstream to bring rain to the thirsty millions, if the people would only respond to the love of a soul who inhabits the sun, who cries at the sight of the parched earth, if gods could be found in moonlight.

☙ ❧

The two trees with the stage monument reappeared, curtains pulled back. There stood someone in a rabbit-suit next to someone in a bear-suit next to someone in a cat-suit. This had a calming effect on the crowds. The rabbit—or more accurately a hare, I am assured—in uniform, delivered a brief epilogue wherein he described the relatively small enclave who called themselves Templars, when they weren't, really. He reassured the audience that the individuals concerned would be arrested and charged, for they were not unknown to the law, but hitherto untouchable. Now they had nowhere to run. There had been one or two old-fashioned scuffles backstage at the PLC.

The three bowed low a few times. They stood still for moment. Then each transitioned into concentric circles of colored beads and trails of lights that wheeled in counterbalancing directions. One by one, they drifted away as on a breeze.

The two curtains closed to present the image of the crop symbol between the trees. A gust from the rising storm brought waves across their surfaces. They billowed, throwing forth the corona of an eclipse that expanded from the symbol in grain until the ring of the sun's light sounded in a rhythmic beat round the dark moon.

The sun set gently, leaving the moon to become a goddess in silhouette, revealed in the shape of a woman. The moonlight from the sun turned her from dark to amber to light, and the last rays clothed her with shadows from the trees. She posed, reflecting the time, like this. Always, this was it. Like this! And like this again. She danced in the sun's vision, for all to see, with their own light. Blue music rose up in the beat of the drums, and she sang in calming tones,

STAY,
PASSENGER. WHY
GOEST THOU BY
SO FAST?

ଓ ଌ

# Epilogue

T—Tiwaz, spear or arrowhead, rune of the god Tyr, defense, justice, law.

It was sometimes customary, I am told, to end an inscription with stacked Tiwaz runes, as above, resembling a tree. Why not? The god Tyr is associated with this rune and with the earliest European democratic assembly, the Thing, often indicated by a local stone circle. In this tradition, the Icelandic Althing shares with the Tynwald of the Isle of Man the distinction of being the oldest surviving parliament.

So that fairly concludes an alphabet of runes, with spearheads arising.

Born in Los Angeles, California, the author grew up among several Western countries. He attended Winchester College in the UK and is a graduate of Amherst College in Massachusetts. He is the cofounder of the Solon Center for Research and Publishing and of EOPA Code Blue Water Solutions.

**Also by Paul V. Cornell du Houx**

**Unicycle, the Book of Fictitious Symmetry and Nonrandom Truth, or the Panpsychist Asymmetry of Nature's Democratic Pi**

Softcover, 2026, ISBN: 978-1-959112-04-4
Hardcover, 2026, ISBN: 978-1-959112-12-9

**"Very scrupulously set out. It is extremely well written and beautifully literate."**

—Dr. Diané Collinson, author of *Plain English*, *Fifty Eastern Thinkers*, coauthor of the *Biographical Dictionary of Twentieth-Century Philosophers*

**"A provocative book by a serious thinker, well worth the reader's time."**

—William A. Haviland, PhD, professor emeritus and founder of the Department of Anthropology, University of Vermont, coauthor of bestselling textbooks, including *Cultural Anthropology* and *Evolution and Prehistory*

**"This book contains some serious mathematics—smart, thought-provoking, and engrossing."**

—William H. Barker, PhD, professor of mathematics, Bowdoin College, coauthor of the textbook *Continuous Symmetry: From Euclid to Klein*

Polar Bear & Company books are available via local bookstores in many countries,
or online,
or at info@soloncenter.org.

Retailers may order via Ingram.

**Yoganomics Sutras**
**on the Transformation Proof:**
**Nature's Panpsychist Balance, the Moral Compass**
**For the Economy**

Softcover, 2026, ISBN: 978-1-959112-06-8
Hardcover, 2026, ISBN: 978-1-959112-09-9

**"[The sutras] act like firecrackers in your intellectual reading consciousness.**

"Cornell du Houx 'developed a math that lets us read the ethics of natural law within the environment.' This is a not inaccurate, but incomplete summary [in the afterword] of *Yoganomics*'s subject matter, which skates an enormous range of philosophical material. [The] afterword characterizes the contents as having 'the ancient and succinct style of the sutra,' indicating the sort of gonglike presence . . . that clearly underpins its ideas.

"For like a sutra, the text consists of numbered sentences . . . some of which have a vatic quality, others plainly conversational. They cover quantum physics, mathematics and pi; politics; various real and figurative modes of addiction; gender; the perils of climate change; the Tao; communist China; Plato; ranked-choice voting; and many more subjects, with recurring focal points involving socioeconomics, nature, environmental degradation, and the dangers of 'absolutes' in everyday thinking."

—Dana Wilde, *Morning Sentinel / Kennebec Journal,*
author of *Nebulae: A Backyard Cosmography*
and *The Other End of the Driveway*

www.ingramcontent.com/pod-product-compliance
Lightning Source LLC
LaVergne TN
LVHW091145080826
845145LV00008B/2268
* 9 7 8 1 9 5 9 1 1 2 0 5 1 *